BETA Reading Deb Day

Proof read/editing by Zeldos

Cover art by Peter Swain, Orphan Press

CHAPTER 1

You have to be comfortable, that's the *numero uno* requirement of any sniper, comfort, and I was very comfortable. The sun shining above me was warm on my back. I was lying prone on dry grass, peering through the low hedgerow of thick scrub in front of me that formed my cover, and my rifle felt easy in my hands. Yes, I was very comfortable lying there on the grassy knoll. Yeah, I know, you're thinking Kennedy now aren't you, eh? Everybody does when you mention grassy knoll. Funny how some words remind us of other things.

Sorry to disappoint you, dear reader, but this grassy knoll isn't the one in Dallas; it's one above the town of Perast in Montenegro that looks down over the red tiled rooftops to the Bay of Kotor, and the small manmade concrete island called Our Lady of the Rock that sits a hundred metres out from the shore in the blue waters of the bay. I could see why so many people came here for their holidays, pure peace and quiet, and I was about to shatter that.

I pushed the barrel of my rifle through the hole I had cut in the hedge and looked out over the shimmering blue water to the island through the rifle's scope. A visitor was clearly expected. A group of men had emerged from the only building on the island, other than the church, and were making their way to the small docking area. Usually small pleasure boats would deposit their tourists at that dock and wait for them to do the disappointing church tour, buy a small but expensive plastic replica and maybe a postcard or two, and then ferry them onto the next scam. I wondered how many holidaymakers knew that the island was a fake, originally made by sinking old ships full of rocks?

But I wasn't on holiday, wish I was. I had a job to do – more to the point, a man to kill. Gold's voice crackled in my ear piece.

'White skiff, five on board, target is in a green jacket. The others look to be security.'

I moved the rifle so the scope picked up the skiff. It was making its way towards the island from the small mainland harbour. The water in the bay was dead calm so the skiff wasn't bobbing about. It was an easy shot. The man in the green jacket looked fairly old, he was sat in the back of the skiff whilst those around him stood; they were much younger, and Gold had got it right, security. You can tell them a mile away, or from my position, just five hundred metres away. Their dark glasses, buzz cut hair and large jackets that no doubt concealed a shoulder holster holding a Glock or PPK47 gave them away, as did the way they stood beside the seated older man, affording him some cover from a sniper. I smiled – sorry chaps, that ain't gonna work. I moved the scope to the mark, his head sat nicely in the cross hairs, I took a deep breath, held it, and squeezed the trigger. I heard the soft phutt of the silencer at the same time as the human head in my sights exploded when my bullet passed through it, disintegrating the bone of the skull and then, judging by the howling coming up from the lake, it must have travelled onwards into one of the goons, lodging in his thigh. I didn't have time to look and find out. Job done, money in the bank, now we get out of here.

'Nice shot,' Gold's voice came through. 'You win anything on the top shelf.'

'I'll settle for a fast car to the airport.' I was already halfway through breaking down the rifle and putting the parts into a canvas shoulder carrier. For a job like this I use a German-made Blaser R39 LRS2 with .338 Lapua Magnum bullets and a suppressor. Pretty hard to get and quite expensive kit, but bloody brilliant to use, and it breaks down into a two foot carrying bag.

I unscrewed the silencer, put it in and zipped up the bag. ‘I’m on my way.’

Now for the dodgy bit; I had to break cover from the protection of the hedge and make it over a twenty metre uphill open area on the knoll that was visible from the bay before I would drop out of view down the other side. One, two, three, go!

I got three quarters of the way up with a zig-zag run before the dry earth around me jumped up in small clouds as bullets from the goons on the skiff zinged up. I’d been spotted. Believe me, reader, when you are running with your back to an enemy who is shooting at you, the only thought in your mind is ‘why didn’t I choose a different career?’ Luckily, precision aiming with a pistol from an unsteady skiff on water over 500 metres away isn’t easy, but all it would take was one lucky shot. They didn’t get one. I dropped over the top of the knoll and stumbled down the other side to the dusty dirt lane at the bottom. Gold was already there astride a motorbike. She had been further down the hill watching the lake, and at the same time watching the lane just in case a tourist wandered up and had to be told *no entry, private property*.

I furrowed my brow at her. ‘I expected a car.’ When we had parted earlier she was going to steal a fast car, something that wouldn't stand out in traffic. Now, I don't pretend to know anything about motorbikes, but this looked a bit of a beast that would turn heads. Then I noticed the blue lights on the back and front. 'Police?'

She nodded. 'He got a little too inquisitive, asked for my passport.'

'Well, you could have showed it to him and he'd have gone away.'

'I did, and he didn't. He decided he was going to check it out on his radio.'

'Where is he?' I knew that once the officer had reached towards his radio button he had signed his own death warrant.

She nodded towards a ditch five metres back off the other side of the road. I took a look. One bullet hole slap bang in the middle of the officer's forehead.

'Come on.' Gold fired the ignition and the bike throbbed into life, deep and full of pent-up energy like a horse in the gate. 'The alarm will have been raised by now, we need to go. You have the helmet, I've got the visor. You can take this too.' She passed me the police helmet and an expensive Burberry shoulder bag, our tool kit. A lady with a Burberry bag hanging from her shoulder wouldn't attract any attention. It had been Gold's idea to use it for our tool kit. Inside there wasn't the usual make-up and hairspray you might expect, but two PKKs, sticks of Semtex, acid fuses, flash-bangs, ammunition, a comms unit, balaclavas, and anything else that the job in hand might find useful.

I took the helmet she offered and put it on and then wore the Burberry like a satchel. I lay my rifle bag across the bike and straddled the pillion with my arms circling her body. They wouldn't have been the first arms to do that. We took the bumpy lane at speed, leaving a trail of dust, and left it as we joined the main road towards the Croatian border. I checked my watch; our flight was due to leave Dubrovnik for Heathrow at 16.30. It was now 13.00, so plenty of time. Things looked good.

My feeling of well-being was interrupted by the vibrating of Woodward's mobile in my pocket. Woodward is the top man at MI6, Britain's foreign intelligence agency. I'll tell you more about him in a minute. Like all the UK's undercover operators, I had been given an ordinary-looking mobile phone that was far from ordinary. It had just one incoming and outgoing line, to and from Woodward. It was satellite-linked, so he could call you and you could call him anywhere in the world.

I released one arm from around Gold and pulled it out. Woodward had sent a text. It wasn't the text I wanted to read: *you got the wrong man.* I held the mobile in front of Gold, chest-high. Her head nodded after she had read it. At the next layby we pulled up.

Gold raised the visor. 'The man you shot was the man registered as Alaric Erdinger at the Perast hotel. The hotel staff called him Mr Erdinger.'

I thought it through; there had obviously been a cock-up somewhere along the line of communication, but not our error. I'd killed the man I'd been sent to kill. Woodward could sort it out; his problem, not mine. 'OK, how far is the Croatian border?'

She shrugged. 'Ten minutes.'

'How long to the airport from there?'

'Two hours maximum.'

I checked my watch. 'Right, let's get back home. Nothing we can do here, and I don't think we'd be welcome back in Perast.'

'Looks like they are missing us already.' Gold nodded back up the road.

In the distance blue lights were flashing. Two black CRV vehicles about a mile away were speeding towards us.

'We can outrun them,' I said. 'Be over the border before they get near us.'

'The border will have been alerted and waiting for us.'

She was right; we'd be the meat in the sandwich, border guards in front of us and these two cars behind.

'Okay, let's get rid of them. You take the front car and I'll take the second one.'

She nodded. I got off the bike, gave her the police helmet, and made my way to the scrub about twenty yards back from the lay-by and knelt behind a thick bush. I checked that my PPK Walther had a full clip and clicked the safety off. Gold had pushed the bike over onto its side and lay beside it, giving the appearance of having lost control and coming off with the helmet on the ground beside her covering her right hand, the hand I knew would be holding her PPK.

Our pursuers took the bait. Both the CRVs halted in a cloud of dust ten metres from the bike and Gold. Their blacked out windows hid the number of occupants, but the accident scenario worked and the doors opened and two occupants from the nearest car and three from the other one jumped out. Our ducks were all in a row. I stepped out from behind the bush, and holding my pistol in a double grip took the nearest goon out, followed by the other two in quick succession. The surprise attack had the two from the front car turn towards me and fumble for their pistols which gave Gold more than enough time to bring out her pistol from beneath the helmet and take them out. It was over in a matter of seconds. Five bodies on the ground and Gold and I in the first CRV racing away down the road towards the Croatian border. She kept the accelerator floored and the blue lights flashing. The Montenegro border guards would have been alerted and be expecting their police or secret service officers or whatever the goons were, so we should be waved straight through; but then five hundred metres further along the road the Croatian Customs post wouldn't be keen on letting a Montenegro Secret Service car drive through.

I rang Woodward and explained. He wasn't happy, but understood there was no going back to Perast. I told him we had nicked a Montenegro police car; I didn't mention the five bodies left in a lay-by.

'Can you get us through Croatia Customs? They're going to ask questions about the car, and if they do a search they'll not be happy.'

‘By that I assume you have an arsenal of weapons in the boot?’

‘Just a few.’ Two PKKs, a sniper rifle and a Burberry full of nasty things weren’t the usual holiday maker’s luggage.

‘How long until you get to the Croatian border?’

‘Ten minutes. I can pull off the road for a while if you need more time. I’m not bothered about the Montenegro border, they’ll be expecting a police car and will wave us through.’

‘Right, get through the Montenegro check point as quick as you can before they realise who is in the police car and stop you. I really don’t want to have to explain to a friendly NATO member what you are doing in their country armed to the teeth. Croatia is fine – if they pull you in before I make some arrangements with the SOA, you just stay quiet and wait whilst they batter you with a lead pipe in a sock and pull out your finger nails.’

I got the impression he was relishing that thought. The line went dead. I took it that the SOA he referred to was the Croatian Security Service.

I was right about the border guards at the Montenegro check point. They were clearly expecting the police car and weren't aware it had been hijacked. They cleared a lane and waved us through. Half a mile further down the road we hit the end of the queue of vehicles being checked through one by one into Croatia. We moved forward slowly, and I hoped Woodward was making progress with our clearance. I pressed the button to lower the electric windows. A large CRV with blacked out windows might make a Croatian border guard carrying an AK-47 a bit jumpy. We edged further forward, just one car in front of us being checked. I noticed Gold had one hand inside her jacket. No doubt her PKK was nestling in it, safety catch off.

I nudged her. 'No.'

She relaxed her hand and put it back onto the steering wheel.

'Passports.'

I hadn't noticed the guard approach from behind. His hand was outstretched towards me. Gold pulled her passport from a pocket as I did the same, and we passed them both out of the window. A second guard joined the first, only this one was much older, and judging by the amount of insignia on his uniform very much a senior officer by rank. He spoke to the younger guard and took the passports off him. The young guard wandered off to the next car behind us. I took the two passports as they were handed back through the window. His English was perfect, his smile broad.

'Mr Woodward sends his regards.'

That was it, nothing else. He stood back, signalled to the guards manning the barrier which was raised, and we didn't need a second invitation as Gold moved the car slowly through the check point and back onto the main road. Next stop, the British Consulate in Dubrovnik to offload our weapons. No way could they get past the sensitive metal detectors of an airport Customs, and even Woodward's contacts wouldn't be able to swing that one! They would be parcelled up at the Consulate and sent back to the UK in the diplomatic bag for me to collect from MI6 headquarters on the Albert Embankment. Handy item is a diplomatic bag. Let's not kid ourselves, every country X-rays every diplomatic bag coming in or going out; but the protocol of non-interference holds firm.

CHAPTER 2

The flight back from Dubrovnik had been uneventful; no last minute hitches at the airport, no being dragged off the plane by goons in balaclavas and slung inside a bare cell and beaten to a pulp. That's for the fiction writers.

There is no truer saying than *'home sweet home'*. I spend a lot of my time, if not too much of my time, in foreign places, but nothing beats having my feet up on a recliner on my fifth floor balcony overlooking the Thames, with the evening sun glowing off the buildings on the opposite embankment. My *home sweet home* being a two-bedroom apartment in a modern serviced block overlooking the Thames and Jubilee Gardens at Waterloo. Costs a bomb, but being a serviced block nobody gets in that doesn't live here, and anybody visiting has to get past the security chaps on the door who ring up for permission first. That way I know who's coming up, and I know who – if anybody – has been asking for me.

I had checked with the door staff when I got back from Croatia; nobody had shown any interest in me. The underground car park also gave a separate way out if I ever needed to leave in a hurry without using the main entrance.

Well, you never know, do you? The final piece of my security was that the apartment was not leased in my name – I was registered as George Hadlow with the landlord. George was the first name I'd come across on a gravestone in a great plague cemetery off the York Road. Nobody would be able to trace him, that's for sure. A man I know does fake passports and credit cards. He provided me with all the documentation and references I needed to secure the lease. The old maxim of '*it's not what you know in this world, it's who you know*' is so true.

I slept well and rose about nine, had a fry-up for breakfast, yes I know, not good for me but sometimes nothing else will do. Then I took a stroll to Waterloo station and did a couple of double backs to make sure I was not being followed, I wasn't, then took a black cab and picked up our *tool kit* that had been sent back in the diplomatic bag to Legoland – that's the name people in the espionage industry call the MI6 HQ; it really does resemble something built with Lego blocks, Google it and see for yourself. And now I was on a recliner on my balcony cleaning and oiling my Blaser R39 sniper rifle ready to put it back, where it belongs, into my secure gun cabinet with my other guns, standing between an

Uzi and an Anscultz .22. One gun for every situation I might be asked to undertake.

Woodward's mobile buzzed. I'd left it on the table by the front door. Blast. I was comfortable on the recliner, and I knew whatever Woodward wanted it wouldn't contribute to my comfort. I put the rifle down and walked through to answer it.

'Drag Queen Clothing Company, how can we help you babe?'

Woodward ignored it; he always does.

Commander Clarence Woodward, although he'd never been in any front line of fire except for maybe a few expletives from the Home Secretary when things in MI6 went wrong, is a civil servant. He had progressed through the Ministry of Defence and then into MI6, quickly climbing the ladder to the top where he had been my boss during the latter part of my N14 service – N14 being the select group of military-trained individuals who do the jobs that even the SAS decline: political hits to assist regime change, destruction of enemy threats and blowing up Soviet nuclear progress installations, things like that. To look at him, you would never know Woodward was anywhere near that stuff; tall but slightly built, dark hair neatly combed back, fawn overcoat, black bowler, pinstriped suit, regimental tie, shining brogues, and always with his umbrella for company, he gave the immediate impression of being *'somebody in the city'*. He doesn't waste words either.

'You shot the wrong man.'

'I'll send an apology to his mum.'

'Alaric Erdinger is in London.'

'Who did I shoot?'

'Alaric Erdinger.'

'Identical twins?' This was beginning to sound like a James Bond movie script.

'No, you shot Alaric Erdinger *Junior*, the son.'

'Erdinger senior won't be too happy then.'

'Happier than being dead.'

'You're not getting the money back.'

'We don't want the money back, Nevis – we want the job done correctly. I'll come to your office at eleven tomorrow with details.'

'No, come to the Concourse.'

I could hear Woodward sigh. 'Must we meet there?'

When I have an active job ongoing, I avoid my office. It's a nice office in a small block in the Borough High Street. No problems there, but it's registered to my private eye company, and so easily found if somebody is looking for me. If those friends of Alaric Erdinger had somehow found out who killed the boy wonder then they might, just might, be waiting for me at the office, or at the very least watching it. So instead I use the concourse cafe on Charing Cross Railway Station for any meetings. It is ideal. A busy little public cafe set at the back of the station from where a table in the window gives me a panoramic view of the concourse and everybody on it. Anybody out of the ordinary, like a hitman from Montenegro coming for me with a machine gun, would stick out a mile. I exaggerate, but you get what I mean.

'Or I could come to *your* office?' I gave him an alternative.

'No, definitely not, I've already had the Foreign Office on my back. They've had the Montenegro Ambassador screaming at them about an assassination in Perast in front of tourists. If anybody connected to the FO is in the building and happens to see you suddenly appearing in my office, two and two will make four and questions will be asked that I do not wish to answer. This is the *Secret* Service, Nevis, and I wish to keep it that way.'

'It's the concourse then.'

He sighed. 'At eleven. Oh, and Nevis..'

‘Yes.’

‘It’s preferable not to sit in public view on your balcony when cleaning a rifle.’

The phone went dead. The bugger had somebody watching me from over the Thames; the spy spying on the spy. I had to admire his thoroughness. I walked out onto the balcony and gave a stiff finger across the Thames.

Woodward’s phone is a unique piece of kit. It has a call and a receive button, that’s all, no keyboard and just the one direct line from anywhere in the world to or from Woodward. I imagine it uses micro satellite technology to bounce a call through time zones and avoid deflection. I hope he doesn’t pay roaming charges on it. I smiled to myself at the thought of him receiving that bill!

I rang Gold and told her of the meeting tomorrow. She would be there; I wouldn’t see her, but she would be there somewhere. That’s her job – she covers my back and carries the Burberry stuffed full with whatever she thinks might be needed for the job in hand.

Alison Gold, nickname Gold Digger – I just call her Gold: five foot eight, late thirties, medium build, hair in a fringe to her neck – sometimes she’s blonde, sometimes brunette, sometimes a redhead – natural brown eyes that would change depending on what colour contact lenses she had in. Overall, Alison is a nice attractive-looking lady, but beneath the well-groomed exterior is another Alison – the Alison whose parents and siblings had been killed in their Ashkelad home by a rocket fired across the Palestinian border from Gaza into Israel by Hamas; the Alison who had refused to be fostered and formed a bad habit back in her teens of gold digging, hitting on wealthy men of a certain age and relieving them not of their sexual urges but of a good proportion of their wealth in cash or expensive gifts in order to live, which is where her nickname came from. She always targeted a married man with a reputation to lose or a 'celeb name', so calling in the police once you'd been duped by the Gold Digger wasn't an option if you wanted to maintain your reputation or fan base; and especially not if the duped one had a wife who might not be very understanding to the situation.

Gold had been conscripted into national service with the Israeli Defence Force and found she liked the life. It gave her security, and the chance of revenge for the loss of her family. She was soon noticed as a bit special and moved into Mossad. She was an ideal fit, exactly what they and most elite military squads look for: a person with no family ties and the ability to make a cool and measured assessment of a situation and then act. That's Alison.

We go back to the Afghan war when the N14 unit I was attached to in 2011 went into Pakistan by Chinook to cover a USA special ops SEAL unit that had been sent in to kill Osama Bin Laden and then had one of their choppers malfunction. Our emergency brief was to blow up the trapped chopper if it couldn't get back in the air and totally destroy Bin Laden's compound – anything of use to an enemy had to be destroyed. We were low on manpower at that time, with many operations against Al Qaeda going on, and help was requested from Mossad to assist us in case the Pakistanis got wind of the operation and came to stop it. The Mossad unit we got was their Kidon unit which specialises in assassinations, originally formed by Golda Meir in 1972 after the Munich Olympics Israeli athlete murders to track and kill every one of the PLO Black September group that had carried out those killings. By 1979 that mission had been accomplished, they'd killed them all, and Kidon was reassigned to assassinate Iranian nuclear scientists and top military generals of the Iran Revolutionary Guard; the latest one being Mohsen Fakhrizadeh, their top nuclear scientist, killed by a machine gun mounted on a truck and operated via a satellite using facial recognition software. Brilliant, eh? It's a long way from a bullet in the head or a slit throat, which were the kill options of choice in my active days.

Anyway, everything went fine at the Bin Laden compound, the USA copter got off the ground and we all fled over the Pakistan border before they could react. At the debriefings Gold and I, as heads of our units, were debriefed together to make sure our stories matched, and then we went our separate ways. I went over the age limit for N14 and was seconded into the Met's Organised Crime Squad, did a stint there, and then moved into the private sector where I am now. Gold ended her association with Kidon as they only use you for three years, and went back to her elite Israeli military group Flotilla 13; finding that didn't set the adrenalin alight after Kidon, she left and went into personal security in London, with a nice sideline by resuming her *gold-digging*. She made one mistake: she targeted one of my top clients, and I quickly sussed her out and stepped in. We recognised each other and became good friends, and sort of business partners; she had skills in the cyber world of IT and the dark web, whilst I could present a pretty hard face to any of her *gold-digger* victims who got nasty. As a reliable back-up, she's second to none – I wouldn't want anybody else.

CHAPTER 3

The next day I got to Charing Cross Station ten minutes early and took a seat at my usual table facing out across the concourse. I gave Gold a call on my mobile.

'Yes.'

'I take it you're here somewhere?' I said, knowing full well she would be.

'Yep, got you covered.'

'Okay, I'll leave my mobile open so you can hear the conversation.' I always do that when Gold's involved, saves repeating everything to her later.

'Okay, have fun.' She's a sarcastic bugger sometimes.

I ordered a coffee from the counter and took it back to my table as Woodward arrived flanked by his two protection officers who took their usual seats at the back wall of the café, trying to be inconspicuous whilst standing out a mile. Woodward nodded a greeting to me and flapped at the plastic chair seat with his leather gloves to remove any crumb that dared to be waiting to attach itself to his Crombie coat. He removed his bowler and sat down.

'Coffee?' I asked.

He gave his usual unspoken answer with a look that said, ‘Do you really think I would let British Rail coffee into my digestive system?’

I carried on. ‘So we hit the wrong member of the family then?’

‘Not your fault, Nevis. Somebody in surveillance got the Erdingers mixed up.’

‘Father and son with the same Christian names, easily done.’

He shot me a slightly angry look. ‘Not in MI6, Nevis – things get double checked.’

‘And this one wasn’t?’

‘No, this one was. It was double checked, and Erdinger Senior was in the hotel the day before, but apparently we now understand he fell ill and Erdinger Junior flew out to take his place at the meeting on the Rock at the last moment’

‘Didn’t your people in Montenegro notice that?’

‘They’d left – once they had seen Erdinger Senior was booked into the hotel their surveillance job was done. Can’t have any of our chaps found in the vicinity of an assassination.’

‘Which is why I got the job.’

‘Exactly.’

‘Because, as you have told me before, I am expendable.’

'Exactly, which is why we pay your extortionate fee.'

'I looked up expendable in the dictionary once, do you know what it said?'

He took a deep breath. 'No, nor do I care.'

'It said, *of relatively little significance, and therefore able to be abandoned or destroyed.'*

'Exactly. I couldn't put it better myself. Now shall we get back to the matter in hand? Erdinger Senior is still the main target, and I would like you to complete the mission.

'I did complete the *mission,* as you call it. I killed the man your people told Gold was staying in a certain Hotel in Montenegro, a man called Erdinger – no description, just a name, and when the man with that name left the hotel the doorman, who had received an amount of money from Gold, tipped her the wink and I carried out the job. Contract fulfilled.'

Woodward took a large breath and sat back in the chair. 'Okay, shall we get to the bottom line, Nevis? How much?'

He knows me so well.

'Where is Erdinger Senior now, still in Montenegro?' I asked.

'No, London.'

'London?'

'Yes, he was in the air on his way back as you were taking aim at his son. Let me tell you a little about the Erdinger family.'

'Family? There's more of them?'

'Not now, no.' He held a hand up to silence my next question. 'The man we are looking to extinguish...'

'You mean kill.'

'Yes, the man we are looking to kill is the son of Field Marshall Barend Erdinger, who was a senior ranking figure in the Stasi.'

'The Stasi?' That was a surprise. 'East German State Security before the wall came down in1989.'

'Quite...'

'So this Field Marshal, he would have been the grandfather of the Alaric Erdinger I killed.'

'Indeed he would.'

'He can't still be alive?'

Woodward took a deep breath and blew it out. 'Please be quiet, Nevis, and let me finish if you would?'

'Okay.'

He regained his posture. 'Field Marshall Barend Erdinger fled when the wall came down, and like most of the other high-ranking Stasi Officials he went to one of the small communist enclaves in Europe or Russia. At the end of the war the Nazis fled to South America, and the Stasi to Europe. Erdinger and his cohorts, backed by the Russians and using looted gold, worked their way into the more democratic Eastern European countries' political systems and over time established a foothold for themselves and their younger followers. They were responsible for maintaining Russian influence in those countries when the Soviet Union collapsed; they advised and mentored people like Lukashenko in Belarus on how to stifle the growing democracy movement there; they formed the backbone of the Russian Transnistria enclave in Moldova and the Donesk region of Ukraine; they hid in the background in Kazakhstan until its independence.' He took another breath. 'They are funded by Putin's FSB, the modern equivalent of the KGB, and Russian money flows into those places through the main Stasi organisation to their local branches, which are known as Pyramids. The Pyramids then pass the money on as bribes to officials, or for assassinations to keep democracy from gaining a foothold and their chosen people into positions of power. They gradually take over the main wealth-creating industries and infrastructure of the country. Field

Marshall Erdinger built those Pyramids and handed over the dictatorial power he held to his son Alaric Erdinger Senior. He was the target in Montenegro, not his son Alaric Erdinger Junior.'

'I take it his son was involved though?'

'Very much so, he was being groomed for control at some stage. But obviously not anymore. So, the power still lies with the father. If we can remove him from the main organisation the Pyramids collapse, which is the reason we sent you to Montenegro. He is the glue holding the organisation together, a man with important contacts and friends in high places. Putin has three children – well, three we know of – and Alaric Erdinger Senior is godfather to two of them. He's trusted, and one of the Kremlin inner circle. Put him out of action and the house of cards will fall, and might even bring the Kremlin down with it.'

'Okay, but aren't you missing something out?' I raised my eyebrows questioningly.

'Missing something out?' Woodward feigned ignorance.

'Yes, nothing you've told me involves us – all Erdinger's dealings are in Europe, none in the UK. Why are you getting involved? Where's the threat?'

Woodward smiled, steepled his fingers and thought for a few moments. 'Erdinger has a connection with the German far right party the AFD. They are very strong, and their membership is growing fast in the old Communist regions of what was East Germany before the wall came down – they have a membership nearing forty thousand, and are even standing a candidate in the next Chancellor election. They are anti-immigration, very racist, and use violence at their rallies against any opposition. They also have a growing youth wing and have taken a whole area of land as an independent state and called it Reichsburger and cut it off from the rest of the country. In 2022 an attempt to overthrow the German Government was foiled by the security services. Russian money is funding them, and guess who is controlling them?'

It was obvious. 'Erdinger.'

'Yes. He recently attended a far right AFD rally and our people who keep an eye on him noticed he brought some guests with him. Guests he had especially flown in from the UK. Guests that included people from far-right groups in the UK, including Patriotic Alternative, National Action, the defunct EDF and others.'

Woodward's interest in Erdinger was becoming clearer.

'So he's putting together something in the UK,' I said. It was a qualified guess.

'Indeed he is, Nevis – he's constructing a Pyramid. He is funding anarchists, donating funds to certain far right MPs, and buying shares in defence and armament associated companies through Belize-based trust funds that will eventually become the prominent share holder in those companies, and legally capable of voting Erdinger's people onto the boards. We can't entertain that, Nevis, it has to be nipped in the bud – and I'm afraid people like Erdinger can't be sensibly persuaded to cease their actions, therefore our only recourse is extinction.'

He has a wonderful way with words.

I smiled. 'Extinction?'

'Yes, Erdinger must go the way of the Dodo.'

My smile turned into laughter.

Woodward permitted himself a smile. 'He is attending a CBI dinner in the Guildhall tomorrow evening, I suggest you start there – and Nevis...' He gave me a cold stare, '...this is all under the table – no fire fights or exploding cars, just a quiet removal of an unwanted guest who is making a nuisance of himself.'

‘Mr Woodward, you can be such a spoilsport.’

‘Indeed I can, Nevis.’ He gathered his gloves and bowler.

‘There’s just one small item we haven’t covered,’ I said.

‘Is there?’

‘Ten thousand.’

Woodward raised his eyebrows. ‘Ten thousand what?’

‘Pounds – ten grand a day plus expenses, and a week upfront for my family in case I don’t make it back.’

‘You don’t have a family, Nevis – if you had you wouldn’t even be considered to work for us. We don’t employ family men. Ten thousand is far too much. You took five for the Montenegro job.’

‘Not if I had known who the mark was. And let’s face it, Erdinger now knows he’s a target and was very nearly a corpse. His security will be so tight it shouts danger to me very loudly. His people will be breaking arms to find out who the hot shot on the hill in Perast was and who he was working for, because whoever planned it knew too much about Erdinger’s movements.’

'True. All right, ten plus expenses, but a time limit of fourteen days.'

'And I want a bonus if the Kremlin falls,' I added with a smile.

He laughed. 'A bonus?'

'Yes, Easter is coming so I'll have an egg.'

'An egg?'

'Yes, a Fabergé egg.'

Woodward ignored the remark, stood and buttoned his coat. 'This is the British Secret Service, Nevis, not the FBI – we don't give bonuses for completing an assignment.' He leant towards me, 'You'll be lucky to get a Cadbury's Cream Egg, let alone a Fabergé one. Good day, Nevis.' He lent forward and spoke into my mobile. 'And good day to you, Miss Gold.'

He turned and nodded to his protection, who left their table and followed him out of the cafe and off across the concourse. I watched until they were swallowed up in the crowds. I like Woodward. Cut him in half and you'll find the St George's Cross running through him like a stick of rock.

I picked up the mobile and spoke to Gold. 'Well, what do you think?'

'I think you should refuse the job if you want to live to see Christmas.'

CHAPTER 4

It was the next day. I walked to my office and gave Gold a call as I turned into the Borough High Street.

‘Good morning. I’m ten minutes away – all quiet?’

‘Good morning to you too. Yes, all quiet. I’ve checked the office – no booby traps on the door, nobody sitting in a car watching it. Seems like Erdinger’s people haven’t located Mr Porton.’

I laughed. When I work for Woodward I use an alias, one of five, all names of UK Military bases: Portman, Cheltenham, Northolt, Lakenbury and Faslane. I have ID and passports for all five, each with different details about the passport owner. I’d used the Mr Henry Portman one to travel into and out of Croatia and Montenegro, so when the Montenegro Security Service or Erdinger’s people traced me through their Customs controls, that is as far as they would have got. Henry Portman took a flight to the UK and then disappeared, ceased to exist. I hope. The only flaw in that system is facial recognition databases. Obviously the picture in the passports has to be me, and if my adversary has access to a facial recognition database that has my mugshot in it I could be in trouble. They'd never find my home address, but the office is registered to my private eye company, and some of these FRDs list work history, especially the various European police and security force ones.

'I'll get coffees from Mehmet's,' I said.

'Good idea.'

Mehmet's Deli, the best deli south of the Thames, with the best doner kebabs in London. I sorted out a bit of trouble his daughter was having with a street bro a while ago. The kid took exception to an *'old man'*, as he called me, telling him to stop pestering the girl as she wasn't interested, and he could do just what he pleased. What he can't do now is run very fast. If you break a kneecap by stamping into it from the front it will break and what the surgeons call 'float'. After that, you limp for the rest of your life. Shame, but I did ask him nicely a couple of times to leave the girl alone. He's not been around Mehmet's since. Yes, I know, using violence isn't a nice way to make your point, but when all else fails... I exchanged greetings with Mehmet and ordered two coffees.

My mobile buzzed in my pocket. It was Gold.

'I suppose you want a cake as well, eh?'

'Maybe later, but right now you have company.' My heart skipped a beat. 'Two men, one in a dark suit and the other in a brown leather jacket and jeans. The dark suit has walked past Mehmet's three times, he's checking if you are still there. I suggest we use the car park.'

'Okay.' The car park was a private underground one three buildings down from my office building. I rent two spaces in it.

Gold continued. 'I'll go and park there now, I'm in the dark blue Kia. You walk down the ramp and hopefully they'll follow. Are you carrying?'

'No.' Why would I carry a gun on my way to work? You live and learn, eh? I will from now on.

'Okay, I'll park at the bottom of the ramp on the right and put a PKK on the top of the front left tyre, safety catch off. I'll be over the other side of the garage and take their attention. I'll take the suit.'

'Got it.' Mehmet was at the coffee machine, and I spun him a lie as I put my phone back in my pocket, 'Sorry, Mehmet, that was my guest – she can't make the meeting so I'll just need one coffee, not two.'

'No problem, Ben.' He passed it over. 'Enjoy.'

I smiled. I knew he wouldn't accept any money, so I stuffed a fiver into his charity box and left. I only took the one coffee because walking out with two would have told the suit and the jacket that I was not alone. Clever, eh? I crossed the road, dodging between the traffic; I couldn't pick out the two goons, but Gold wouldn't be wrong, they'd be around somewhere. I was pretty safe in the open on the street; they wouldn't shoot in public if that was what they were sent to do, more likely they would want details of who was running me before they killed me. I kept an eye on my image mirrored in the shop windows, just in case anybody got too close, but nobody did.

I turned into the car park and walked down the ramp. Gold's Kia was parked five cars down on the right, so she would be on the left somewhere. I stopped by the nearside front wheel and put the coffee on the bonnet; my followers would be quickening their pace now, thinking the Kia might be mine and I was about to drive away. I knelt and pulled the pistol from its resting place on top of the tyre and swung round in one movement. A single shot rang out as the two followers came into my view and the suit crumpled to the floor, his gun spinning away. As the jacket turned to where Gold's shot had come from, I sent a .45 across the twenty metres between him and me into the back of his head. His gun clattered to the ground and he fell beside it. Silence and stillness settled on the car park. I gave it ten seconds, just in case there was a third member of the goon's team backing them up. Nothing, nobody came running in from the street.

'Clear?' I shouted to Gold.

'Clear,' came back the answer.

After so many similar scenarios, we knew what to do. The two bodies were quickly dragged behind the cars to the far corner of the car park and pushed beneath the back ends of the furthest two. Their drivers would not notice them and drive off unaware of what they had uncovered. The goons' clothes had no papers or ID, very professional, so we took their two pistols and hid them under a blanket in the Kia's boot. They'd be dropped off a bridge into the Thames at some point. I took the coffee from the bonnet and offered it to Gold. She declined, so I drank it.

Gold drove out of the garage to park up elsewhere. When the bodies were found the owners of cars parked in the garage would be hauled in for questioning, not something she wanted to be part of. I walked out and strolled along and into my office building, took the lift to the floor above mine and came softly down the fire escape stairs to check nobody was waiting in the corridor; they weren't. I took a good look at my office door before I put the key in the lock, just to make sure that turning it didn't complete the circuit to a bomb inside. It didn't.

I like my office, it's nice and it's minimalistic – well, it is since Gold threw out the heap of brown furniture I got for a song at the local auction house that used to fill it and bought me a desk, three chairs and a filing cabinet that cost a fortune from some Swedish company that delivered them in flat packs. I won't tell you, dear reader, how many times my stress level hit the roof assembling those flat packs, as no doubt you will have had similar experiences. If you ever see a photo of the CEO of IKEA with a black eye, you will know I have taken my revenge! I have a main office with a smaller office off it which is not used, a kitchen and a WC and washroom.

I settled behind the desk as Gold came in. She didn't look happy.

'Are you fucking mad?' She wasn't happy, she only swears when no other words will do. 'They obviously know who you are and where you can be found, so is it the sensible thing to doto sit behind the desk in your office and wait for the next goon to pop a pistol round the door and shoot you?'

There was only one answer. 'No.'

'Why have you come here in any case?'

'Pick up the mail.'

'Was there any?'

'No.' There seldom is. People wanting to hire a private eye usually phone for an appointment or just turn up.

'Out.'

I could kick myself; a basic error. I got up and followed her out, shutting and locking the door behind me.

'Back stairs,' she said, leading the way along the corridor and onto the fire escape stairs. We split at the bottom and left separately, meeting in Mehmet's.

'So your guest has arrived, eh?' He smiled. 'Coffee?'

'Please, Mehmet. You want to eat?' I asked Gold. 'Best doner kebabs south of the Thames.'

'And north of the Thames too,' added Mehmet with a laugh.

'That would be nice,' said Gold.

‘Two small doners then please, Mehmet.’

I knew we’d get two large ones with all the trimmings, and we did.

‘Right.’ Gold was down to business. ‘What’s the plan? Woodward said Erdinger is going to some CBI thing at the Guildhall this evening. We also know he and his people know there’s a shooter after him and they know it’s you.’

I agreed. ‘Woodward wants this done quietly – no fuss, no media – so that rules out doing it at the Guildhall. Even if I could get in and near to him.’

‘Right.’ She took a bite of the kebab. ‘You were right, this is the best kebab, delicious. Anyway, I suggest we get a trace on Erdinger at the Guildhall and find out where he’s staying in London and work from there.’

Our meal was interrupted by the sound of police sirens approaching. We watched as two patrol cars stopped outside the underground car park and the officers were approached by a man from inside, who pointed down into the gloom.

‘Looks like our earlier work has been found,’ I said as an ambulance arrived.

We carried on with our meal as the car park was sealed off with crime scene tape to keep a growing crowd back. No bodies had been brought out two plain police vehicles with plain clothes officers had arrived followed by a CSI van. Mehmet came to the table and refilled our coffees.

I nodded to the scene across the road. 'What's going on over there, Mehmet?' His customers would have told him the news.

'Two bodies in the car park, probably a drug deal gone wrong. Nobody allowed to move their cars. You park there, don't you?'

'Usually yes, not today. I walked in.' I patted my stomach. 'Too many of your kebabs, got to lose weight.'

I didn't hear his next words as my full attention turned to another plain police car that had arrived, and I recognised the man who got out. Dick Clancy, or to give him his full title, Detective Chief Superintendent Richard Clancy, top honcho in the Met's Organised Crime Squad and my boss for the ten years I spent in OC after I left N14. Since I went private, Clancy has put quite a lot of work my way, mainly standard surveillance but a few hits that had to be made *off piste* as the saying in the Squad goes; in other words, by somebody that can't be connected back to them if anything goes wrong, somebody like me who will pull the trigger for money and ask no questions. But I was asking myself a question now – why was *he* interested in those two bodies?

Gold interrupted my thoughts. ‘We need to sort out a plan for tonight.’

CHAPTER 5

Darkness was draping a blanket over the day as Gold and I, in our black working clothes, sat in the Kia parked in Gresham Street across the road from the flagstone dropping-off area for the Guildhall. I checked my watch: eight o'clock. We had been there since seven to make sure we got a spot where the entrance was clearly visible. Gold checked each car as it pulled up and the people it dropped off through binoculars. The CBI do was obviously a big event; flunkies stepped forward to open the car doors as the shiny limos pulled up one after another, and others queued waiting to disgorge their passengers. As yet no Erdinger had appeared. I was bored; surveillance is a pretty boring job, and I've done a fair bit of it. Mainly for husbands checking on their wives' affairs or vice versa. Easy work, and it pays well.

'Oh very nice,' Gold spoke. 'Very nice indeed. Burgundy Range Rover pulling in now.'

She passed me the binoculars. One of the doormen moved out and opened the back passenger door of the car, and out stepped our man Alaric Erdinger; evening suit, bow tie and walking cane. Woodward hadn't mentioned Erdinger used a walking cane. I'd give you even odds it had a rather nasty blade inside. I passed the binoculars back and delved into Gold's Burberry shoulder bag that was on the floor by my feet, and pulled out a magnetic tracker before slipping out of the car.

'Won't be long.'

I kept the Range Rover in view as it slowly left the drop-off point and edged out into Gresham Street and did a double left into Basinghall Street, which had been closed to traffic and was serving as a car park for the evening. The chauffeur moved it slowly along and joined the end of a long line of parked limos waiting for the call to pick up their owners when the event finished. It would be a couple of hours at least for them to exchange stories, grab a burger from an enterprising mobile burger van parked nearby, or even have a sleep. I melted into the shadows and waited, and watched. Erdinger's chauffeur had the interior light on and was reading a paper. I moved along and walked by on the other side of the road; it was the Evening Standard – good, wouldn't take him long to get through that. It took less time than I thought. Hunger pangs, or the smell of a tasty burger drifting bye must have jabbed his stomach, as he folded the paper, left the car and made his way to join the small crowd of drivers around the burger van fifty metres up the road. I crossed the road, checked nobody was sitting in the car parked behind the Range Rover, clicked the on switch on the magnetic tracker, knelt down and parked it inside the rear nearside wheel arch. Job done.

I felt the cold tip of a pistol barrel placed against the back of my neck and automatically raised my arms.

'Stand up, Mr Nevis.' The voice had an Eastern European lilt.

I stood and turned round slowly. I had a chance, there was just the one of them. Mid-thirties, long dark overcoat, black hair swept back, and a Glock pistol pointing at my head from four feet away.

He snarled. 'I would kill you now, like you kill two of my comrades, but Mr Erdinger would like to talk to you.' He laughed. 'And then I kill you.'

His face registered a look of utter surprise, and his body jumped a little forward before it crumpled to the ground, revealing Gold standing just behind. The short handle of the eight-inch blade she had plunged through his back into his heart stood upright from his dark overcoat, glinting in the amber street light. She leant and pulled it out, wiping the blood from the blade on the goon's overcoat before slipping it back into its sheath on her right ankle.

'He followed you from the square. Two of them watching from a dead end alleyway between two buildings, I clocked them after you left the car.'

'Two?'

'Yes.'

'And the other one?'

'Still in the alley, he won't be going anywhere.'

The inference was clear. He was dead as well.

'We can't leave this one here.'

'He can go back and join his friend in the alley.'

****

The policeman on car parking duty at the end of Basinghall Street gave a laugh as we passed by on the other side of the road with our friend held up between us.

'Getting married in the morning and had a bit too much to celebrate,' I shouted across to him, making a drinking movement with one hand.

The policeman nodded.

We turned up Gresham Street and into the alleyway that was only twenty metres from the Kia. Gold had left the second goon out of sight beside a row of large wheelie bins waiting for the early morning rubbish collection.

'Change of plan, we can't leave them here,' I said.

'Why not?'

'Two bodies in the Borough car park and another two here? The media will have a field day and Woodward will go berserk. It'll be obvious to him that it's us. Put them in the Kia boot and we'll pay a visit to the magicians.'

She nodded that she understood, and we dragged the bodies to the Kia.

CHAPTER 6

The magicians, so-called because they make things disappear – and in the case of these two it is usually bodies – are two brothers in their eighties who operate a South London crematorium for the Council during the day, and run it for the dark side of humanity at night with a *cash and no questions asked* service. Their past is a bit blurred, and I know better than to ask. I was introduced to them and their nocturnal services many years ago by a London mob boss, Jimmy Hanson, whose wife was kidnapped by a very silly pair of young thugs trying to make a name for themselves, and who only succeeded in making themselves dead and departed with 9mm bullets from my PKK in both their heads. I was going to weigh down their bodies and drop them a couple of miles off shore in the Channel, which was the usual procedure in those days, but the boss had used the magicians before and my business association with them began. Sometimes a body dropped in the Channel can wash up on shore and be identified, but it's not likely to pop up from an eleven hundred degree Celsius gas oven. After that first visit I had to take the ashes back to the mob boss in two small coffin-shaped caskets, and he then made a great show of dropping them in the Thames from London Bridge as a warning to any other young upstarts looking to challenge his authority. As far as I know nobody else has, and Jimmy Hanson has gone from strength to strength, and now controls the drug trade in most of London. A very wealthy man.

****

With both the goons' bodies in the boot, Gold headed for South London. I gave the magicians a call on my mobile. It rang a few times before a gruff voice answered.

'Mr Nevis, do you know what time of night it is?' He obviously had my name listed against the incoming call number. 'My brother and I had our cocoa an hour ago and had retired to our beds. I take it the reason for this call interrupting our slumber is that you have a package needing emergency attention?'

'Two packages.'

'Two? My word, you have been busy.'

'It's an unplanned result of a job, and as such I hope you and your brother will be okay with waiting until tomorrow morning for payment? ATMs have a two hundred pound limit, and I'm sure your fee will exceed that.'

'Credit, Mr Nevis? Tut tut. Not something we have ever given.'

'I think my past business with you should stand me in good stead until the morning when I can get to the bank?'

'One moment please, my brother and I will have to talk.'

I could hear mumblings between the two of them. If he said no, then Gold would have to divert to the nearest Thames Bridge, and our friends in the boot would have a watery grave. He came back on the line. 'I think we can reach an agreement, Mr Nevis. Taking into account your past business with us, my brother and I will do the job with payment delayed until the morning. However, considering the late hour, lack of preparation time, and there being two packages as well as a request for credit, it will be fifteen thousand pounds.'

That shook me. 'Fifteen? It was ten for two last time?'

'Ah yes, but Mr Putin has caused a doubling of gas prices since then – blame him, not us.'

'You don't do a *buy one get one free deal*, do you?' I laughed. I didn't have a chance really; the bodies had to disappear for good, and the magicians had the means to make that happen.

He laughed too. ‘No, we don’t do any deals, Mr Nevis – but we are reliable.’ He knew he’d got me by the short and curlies.

‘Okay, we should be with you in thirty minutes.’

‘We? Does that mean you have the lovely Miss Gold with you?’

‘It does, yes.’

‘Ah, well, that makes getting out of bed in the middle of the night worthwhile.’

‘Worth a discount?’

‘No.’

And he rang off.

South London was quite busy on the roads, which I liked – you just mingle with the traffic. The worst time is in the early hours when the roads are empty and the police patrol cars have nothing to do except make some lame excuse to pull over an expensive car with a young lady driver.

We pulled up at the back gate of the crematorium and I gave the brothers a call. The automatic gates swung open and we drove in and around the back of the building, out of sight from the road. They were waiting at the back door, which was open and throwing a wide light onto the gravel yard.

'Make their wishes come true,' I said to Gold.

She laughed and unzipped the cat suit a few inches from the collar to reveal a black lace bra.

'That's far enough,' I said. 'Don't want to have two heart attacks on our hands.'

I got out and opened the boot as the brother with the limp pulled a hospital body trolley from inside and pushed it to the back of the car. The two of them with the trolley clanking across the gravel in the light reminded me of a Hammer Horror film. Gold came round and gave them a smile. That was it – all help in unloading the bodies evaporated as two old men tried to keep their eyes and hands off her without success. I got the bodies on the trolley and pushed it to the doorway as they made inane conversation with Gold, who flirted with them, tweaked their cheeks and pushed their hands away.

'Right, all done. Thanks for your help,' I said sarcastically.' I'm not bringing her next time.'

'You won't get in,' said the non-limp.

We all laughed and said our goodbyes. I promised them the money in the morning, and they promised the job would be done immediately.

We pulled out of the yard and the steel gates clanked shut behind us. I had Gold pull up at the side of the road two hundred metres away, and we turned and watched the crematorium chimney. They were as good as their word; after ten minutes white smoke puffed out, and the two goons were gone for ever.

Gold dropped me off in Streatham and I got a cab home. I presume she went home too. I don’t know where she lives, never asked, and she doesn’t know my home address either.

CHAPTER 7

'The *what* embassy?'

I rubbed the sleep out of my eyes; my fake Rolex on the bedside table showed seven a.m. Gold was on the mobile.

'Angolan Embassy in Dorset Street. Just round the back of Marble Arch. The tracker info sent to my laptop showed Erdinger's car stopped there briefly after the Guildhall thing was over, probably to let him out, as it then went and parked up in a private car park round the corner in Clay Street.'

'Is it still there?'

'Yes, I'm looking at it now. I've swapped the tracker over to one that sends the info direct to an app on my phone.'

The sleep was clearing from my brain. 'You did say the Angolan Embassy, didn't you?'

'Yes.'

'What's Erdinger doing there?'

'Diamonds?'

She was probably right. Angola is Africa's biggest exporter of diamonds, and with only forty percent of the land tested for the precious mineral, it is a magnet for legal and illegal mining. In 2022 the world's largest pink diamond was found there, a one hundred and seventy carat stone they named the Lulo Rose, which started another rush of illegal mines. The thing is that there are just two items that can be traded illegally and used as money in every country in the world, with no questions asked: gold and diamonds. It would cost Erdinger a great deal of money setting up and maintaining his Pyramids; cash is traceable, diamonds are not – and let's face it, the government of Angola isn't known for honesty, and bribery of government officials is the way they work now, and always have. I put two and two together in my head: Erdinger's Pyramid was probably well entrenched in Angola and paid itself in diamonds, which he could use to finance his other Pyramids. Gold was right, and if his car went there after the Guildhall event and then parked up close by, he was probably staying there.

I agreed with her. 'Yes, got to be diamonds, no other reason why he's involved with them.'

'Our next move then?'

'Well, we can't take him out in the Embassy. We'll just have to play a waiting game. I'm going to get a different car. If Erdinger's people know my name and office address they may know what car I drive, and I wouldn't put it past an organisation like his not to have access to the NPR system.'

She agreed. 'Better safe than sorry. They don't have details of mine – if they did they would have shot us inside it last night.'

'Right then, I'll sort out a car and then I have another call to make, and I'll meet you at the concourse at midday.'

'Okay. If the tracker moves I'll let you know.'

'You going to stay there?'

She laughed. 'No, no way – got some business to attend to.'

I didn't ask questions; I knew Gold was still operating her 'gold-digger' business, and the less I knew about that the better. Some wealthy elite man was about to part with a lot of money.

'Okay, see you later.'

Her phone clicked off. Almost immediately Woodward's buzzed. I picked it up and answered.

'House of Lords Pole Dancing Club, what is your membership number?'

He ignored it as he always does. 'Nevis, I seem to remember asking you to make *a quiet removal of an unwanted guest who is making a nuisance of himself.* I fail to see how two bodies in your personal office car park fulfils that criteria?'

'No idea what you are talking about, Mr Woodward. I was at my crochet class all day.'

He ignored me. 'Thankfully neither of the deceased have diplomatic immunity or are registered with any Embassy, and the police are putting a spin on the affair that it was two drug gangs fighting over territory. I would be grateful if in future you would keep within the agreed parameters of the job, Nevis. I suggest you take a look at the television news.' And he rang off.

I took a look at Sky News; the killings were all over it, the usual ex-coppers being interviewed for their opinion. Funny how detectives who couldn't catch a cold when they were in the force become the *go-to experts* when they leave, I switched to the BBC – same thing, different *experts*. Well, I'd things to do, so a shower, bowl of bran flakes with walnuts, a cup of French coffee, and then on with a pair of casual trousers and a light jacket and off to work. I rang for an Uber to pick me up a hundred metres down the road at a junction. That way I never give out my address.

Next I opened my wall safe and took out the magicians' fee, plus a few hundred more for working capital. First stop was the crematorium, which brought a wide smile to their faces at the back gate as the envelope was handed over, and an invitation to be their guest at anytime, as long as Miss Gold was with me. Next stop Deptford Scrap Yard, buyers of ferrous and non-ferrous metals. The yard has a half acre plot at the back of the Deptford industrial estate in South London that backs down to the edge of the Thames – be worth a fortune to a property developer. I paid the Uber off outside the tall corrugated iron gates and walked in past the three chained-off parking spaces in front of a large sign marked *visitors* at the bottom of a concrete set of steps and up to the portacabin office. The sign was actually spelt *visiters* – primary education in Deptford has never been very good.

The site was busy; mobile cranes pulled written off cars from a five deep row and dropped them into a crusher. The cubes of metal that emerged after crushing were lifted onto a row of six deep cubes waiting to be hauled off and loaded onto a freighter at the nearby docks on their way overseas. The whole operation was slick and run by Annie Greggs a chain-smoking Cockney lady, the epitome of mutton dressed as lamb. A couple of years past seventy, she wore an ill-fitting blonde wig, make-up she must put on with a trowel, medically-enhanced 'duck' lips, Botox-enhanced cheeks, breast implants to shame Dolly Parton, and she wore tight tank tops, miniskirts, fishnet stockings and high heel boots. That's Annie Greggs, the epitome of a slapper, and I'd trust her with my life.

She'd inherited the yard from her father who somehow ended up in his own crusher. She'd always maintained he'd slipped on the edge when a gear got stuck and he was trying to release it; others say he welshed on a debt to somebody he shouldn't have and paid the price. I don't know the truth, but I do know that Annie is good at what she does; doesn't suffer fools, and has been known to lay out a twenty-stone docker who ridiculed her appearance with just one right-hander. She and I go back a few years.

The portacabin door opened and the apparition that is Annie Greggs appeared. If we had been in Lourdes the crowd would have fallen to their knees, or more likely crapped themselves, turned on their heels and run a mile. Today her appearance was a bright orange Mary Quant wig that framed an overly made-up face, red leather miniskirt, fishnet stockings that sagged, knee high velvet boots and a blouse that just about kept her enlarged boobs in check. I waited for the words of wisdom to fall from her mouth, a mouth which a shaky hand on the lipstick had enlarged an inch one side and two inches the other.

‘Well, well, well, what the fuck do you want, Ben? I don’t see you for fucking months and then you ping back like a cunt on elastic.’

She has a way with words.

‘I need a car Annie,’ I said as I mounted the steps.

‘And I need a husband, Ben – perhaps we could come to some arrangement?’

I gave her a hug and a peck on the cheek. The hug was a mistake. Her arms glued me to her body and she rotated her lower parts against me. I managed to extricate myself and she laughed. ‘Come on inside, coffee’s made’

Inside the portacabin Annie’s latest toy boy slouched on an old armchair playing a game on his phone. He threw me a quick glance, and Annie couldn’t be bothered to introduce us. He looked just about legal age, jeans and trainers and no future. He would be lucky to last a couple of months as Annie’s pampered pet and be cast adrift like all the others before him. I gave Annie a resigned look and shrugged my shoulders.

'Can't have all work and no play, Ben – got to have some amusement in life. You can take his place if you like?'

'Maybe one day, Annie – bit busy right now.'

'Promises, promises.'

She poured a coffee from the percolator that was always on and passed it over with a plastic bottle of milk.

Somebody was missing: Jimmy Blunt, a seventy-year-old ex-bouncer who acted as Annie's minder, not that she needed one. He was usually sprawled on the sofa, checking the Racing Times to see how far down the field his *dead certs* had finished the day before. I had known Jimmy for years and had given him work collecting money for my clients on a couple of occasions many moons ago, when I was just starting out as a PI and was too busy with a case to handle it myself. Last time I had seen Jimmy was here at Annie's over six months ago and he was in a bad state. He could hardly walk and needed a knee replacement, but there was a three year wait at the NHS – isn't there always? I had a bit of an unexpected cash bonus come my way on a job that I was already being well paid for, and gave Jimmy the money to get his knee done. Annie was charged with making sure that the money went on the operation and not on the horses.

'Jimmy left you?' I asked.

She laughed. 'He'll be back, silly old cunt.'

'Run off with the knee money, has he?' That didn't seem like Jimmy.

'Nah, he had the operation – worked a treat, he was bouncing about on his new knee like a good 'un. Really perked him up, out and about like a new man.'

'And then...?'

'Met a tart twenty years younger than him and moved in with her over Croydon way. Silly old fool. He told her he paid twenty grand for the operation, so she thinks he's got money. She's got a big surprise coming. She'll either kick him out, or the amount of Viagra he must be taking to keep her happy will kill him.' She laughed. 'So what motor are you after?'

'Two litre, reliable and registered.'

Annie gets a lot of cars in her yard – insurance write-offs, unpaid finance repossessions and part exchanges the garages don't want. She took a chain of car keys off a hook on the wall and we left the cabin and walked down the yard to the far end, round the back of a massive heap of twisted metal waiting to be sorted and cubed. It was here she keeps her 'runners', the motors that her mechanic has worked on that run well and are reliable. Each one has a false number plate which is a copy of a legal one registered to some unsuspecting owner. If a nosy police patrol check it on the DVLA database, it will show up as legal and taxed. Easy scam eh? Annie makes money off the 'runners' by renting them out to drug dealers doing their rounds, on a daily basis at some exorbitant rate that I was about to be quoted.

'A ton a day, a monkey a week.'

That's a hundred pounds a day, or five hundred a week to you and me. I was expecting more; Annie is not known for her generosity. She gave me a nudge. 'We could get in the back and negotiate a discount?'

'Don't you ever stop, Annie?' I laughed.

'Got to take every opportunity, Ben – not many years left in the old ticker now.'

I pointed to a Honda CRV. I used to have one before my current Range Rover – good car, reliable and comfy. 'What about that one? It looks okay.'

'Finance repo, too old to sell again. Two litre, petrol – good runner.'

'That'll do.'

I counted out five hundred as she sorted out the key off the chain and we exchanged. I got in and the motor started first turn of the key. I purposely kept my foot off the clutch as I forced the gear stick into first with a loud rasping crunch, and then I pressed the clutch.

Annie looked at me, then shook her head and laughed. 'You bastard.'

She knew all the tricks. She was right, it was a good runner – bit loose on the accelerator but nippy, and no play on the steering. The distinct aroma of cannabis told me what it had been used for on its last outing. I kept the front windows open as I drove out of Annie's yard, hoping I wasn't stopped. I was going to pay Dick Clancy a visit at West End Central police station in Harley Street and ask why Organised Crime were interested in two dead goons in the Borough car park, and why the main man, him, was there. But I only got as far as Kennington when Gold was on the mobile.

'He's on the move.'

'Go on.'

'The chauffeur fetched the car to the Embassy and he jumped in with two heavies and we are off. I'll follow on the tracker – don't want to get too near after last night, they'll be ultra-sensitive and jumpy. They are heading west.'

'I'm at Kennington so should tag on pretty soon.'

'Did you get a car?'

'Fifteen-year-old Honda CRV, quite comfy really.'

'We are in Knightsbridge, just passed Harrods. You know what I'm thinking?'

'Same as me – he's going to Heathrow.'

'Yes.'

'Got the Burberry with you?'

'Of course.'

That was good news; if Erdinger took a flight we'd need our passports. The rest of the toolkit wouldn't get through Customs and would have to be put into a left luggage locker, but we would be able to follow him. I swung over Battersea Bridge and headed for the Westway. All was quiet for a minute before Gold spoke again.

'We've come to a halt.'

'Why?'

'Just Stop Oil are in the road blocking it. I can see Erdinger's car about fifteen feet in front of me – a burgundy Range Rover isn't very good for blending into the surroundings.'

'I'll be on the motorway before you.'

'Yes, probably. The police have arrived and are pulling them off the road, so we should be on the move in a few minutes. I've checked the flights to Angola from Heathrow. They're pretty regular, next one is an Emirates Airline to Luanda at 16.00 – two and a half hours, Terminal Three.'

'I'm going to put my foot down and get there before you. If we both follow him we will have to find parking. He's just going to jump out at the Departures entrance and disappear by the time we park and get in the terminal.'

'Good idea – we are still stationary, there's more protesters than police at the moment. Every time they remove one another takes their place. Some of the motorists are wading in and pulling them off – it's all getting a bit tetchy.'

'That's fine, gives me more time.'

A couple of minutes later I hit the Westway elevated section and floored the accelerator as it opened out to the M4. If your 'good runner' blows up now, Annie Greggs, I'll not be a happy bunny.

As this was hopefully going to be a *find and eliminate* job rather than a *find and bring back* job, I needed some special equipment; and my '*go to*' man for all this kind of thing was

Gilbert Charles. Gilbert has a Gunsmiths in St Martin's Lane off Trafalgar Square, and officially caters for the elite grouse-shooting public school dickheads who take great joy in blasting life out of the sky in the name of sport. Unofficially, Gilbert, always resplendent in his Prince of Wales check jacket, cavalry twill trousers, bow tie and shiny brown brogues, is the top man for things like explosives, rented shotguns, fake IDs, fake passports, and any other items that shouldn't really be on the market; he's a sort of retail dark web. He certainly looks the part of a country gent with an enlarged colour framed photo hanging on the wall behind the mahogany shop counter of himself, a Springer with a grouse in its mouth, a 'broken' shotgun over his arm and a large Tudor country pile behind him; the photo actually having been put together by his own hand in the dark room at the back of the shop that he uses for developing fake ID photos.

A fake ancestral family tree inscribed on parchment behind glass in a mahogany frame hangs beside the photo that traces Gilbert's blue blood line back to 1066, with all of his ancestors being military officers; in reality, the only blue blood Gilbert has in him is from a fountain pen an inmate in the Scrubs stabbed him with after taking offence at his false posh accent. In real life, Gilbert's dad was a bookie's runner in Liverpool and his mother a clippie on the Mersey Corporation buses. Anything of the family history before then is unknown, and as for living in a large Tudor mansion Gilbert has spent more time living at Her Majesty's Pleasure in various government 'mansions' around the country than he has as a free man. Like most of the con artists in our world, it's all smoke and mirrors. I gave him a call on the mobile as I went up the M4.

'Mr Nevis, to what do I owe the pleasure of this call?'

Another person with my number on their call log. Yes, I think maybe it's time to dump the mobile and use burners.

'Hello, Gilbert – you can drop the posh accent. Got a minute to put an order together?'

'Yeah, shop's empty, Ben. I didn't think inflation would hurt the assholes I get in here, but trade's definitely down. You okay? Still wreaking fucking havoc wherever you go?' He laughed.

'You've got the wrong man, Gilbert. I'm a peace-loving social worker.'

'Are you bollocks – right, what do you need?'

‘Well, first off I need to have this on account, because I’m just about to fly out of the country. Is that okay?’ Gilbert had always been good that way in the past.

‘No problem – if you come back in a body bag I’ll sue your estate. Fire away.’

I gave him a list: six eight-inch Semtex sticks, six digital plug-timed detonators, six flash grenades, two smoke bombs, two Walther PKKs and a box of two hundred bullets. ‘Can you manage that?’

‘No problem. I take it you’ll need the usual delivery?’

‘Please.’

‘Okay, I’ll box it up and get the box over within an hour.’

‘You’re a star, Gilbert.’

‘I know, now piss off and let me put it together. Enjoy wherever you are off to – send me a postcard.’ He laughed. ‘See you when you get back, Ben.’

The phone went dead. Gilbert knew the drill; he would pack my shopping list in a sturdy box and deliver them to Woodward at Legoland.

I called Woodward on his direct line. He answered immediately.

‘Yes, Nevis?’

‘Two things – first off, I need you to check a Heathrow passenger list.’

‘Go on.’

‘Emirates flight at 16.00 to Luanda, passenger by the name of Erdinger.’

Silence.

‘Did you get that?’

‘Yes, be right back to you.’ Click, the line went dead.

I needed to check that Erdinger was flying out. I would look a bit stupid standing in Terminal 3 holding two tickets to Luanda when Erdinger drives straight by on the motorway and goes to visit his old mum in Bristol or somewhere similar.

Woodward came back a few minutes later.

‘He is listed. Are you following him?’

‘Yes, he spent the night at the Angolan Embassy. There’s a connection there somewhere.’

‘Nevis, we have a good relationship with Angola – oil rich country. Try and stay under the radar.’

‘Diamond rich too, especially illegally mined ones.’

There was a brief silence. 'I see where you are going with this. And the second thing, you said two things?'

'There's a box of goodies being delivered to you in about an hour. Can you get it on the diplomatic bag list to the Embassy in Luanda as soon as possible?'

'Okay, I'll let you know when they have it. Anything else?'

'That's all.'

Click, and he was gone – not even a 'take care'. He won't get a postcard.

CHAPTER 8

I sat in the Terminal 3 McDonald's where I could see the Emirates check-in desk. I had parked up, topped up my cash from an ATM and bought two tickets to Luanda: one for Gold on Erdinger's flight and one for me on an Air France flight leaving thirty minutes later. I couldn't risk being seen on his flight and identified by one of his goons. Gold joined me five minutes after Erdinger and his protection had gone through check-in. I gave her the Emirates ticket and five hundred pounds and explained that I'd be following.

She reached into the Burberry tool kit. 'Here, this will get through Customs.'

She gave me a passport; I was Mr Lakenheath. I keep one passport in the tool kit for emergencies. She also pulled out an ear piece, clip mic and belt battery for our wireless communications; she would have the same. It was the only thing we could take with us from our tool kit; most Customs officials think it's just a common or garden radio or mobile phone accessory and don't take a close look.

'Right.' She stood and slung the Burberry over her shoulder. 'See you in Luanda.'

I watched as she sailed through check-in. I checked the departure board; her flight was *boarding*, mine was showing.

CHAPTER 9

Quatro de Fevereiro airport in Luanda is the main airport in Angola; the others are very small and far away from the main city. A third of the Angolan population live in Luanda – that's twenty million souls in one city, and two-thirds of them are in favelas, unauthorised slums with no utilities and no law. The whole city throbs with activity; it is very modern with skyscraper office blocks, a holiday beach, a good transport system and a lot of money sloshing around – a great deal of it from the Chinese who have bribed their way in with promises of infrastructure renewal, and no doubt back handers into the Swiss accounts of the ruling class. It's the same throughout Africa; the rich get richer, and the poor get poorer. I suppose that's the same the world over really. I try not to think about it; I'm a killer, not a politician. Mind you, not much difference really when you look at people like Putin and Netanyahu.

I left the airport, connected up my comms and called Gold.

'You made it then,' she said.

'Yes, you too. How was the flight?'

‘No problem, Erdinger spent most of it asleep. Where are you?

‘Outside the Arrivals gate at the airport.’

‘Stay there and I’ll pick you up.’

‘What car have you got?

‘Suzuki Jimny’

I’d never heard of it and waited at the long kerb outside the arrivals, waving away the street sellers. Gold pulled up in the two door car – a sort of mini Range Rover copy, much smaller but the same shape. I got in.

‘Where did you get this, a toy shop?’

‘It’s the biggest selling car in Angola.’

‘Nick it?’ I asked.

‘No, rental. Didn’t you notice that every other kiosk in the main arrivals is a car rental? Quick look at my passport and when I got out dollars to pay the man couldn’t get the paperwork done quick enough.’

‘Where did you get dollars?’

‘There are four currency exchange kiosks in main Arrivals as well. Got a good rate for sterling.’

The currency in Angola is the kwanza – yeah, I know, you’ve never heard of it. Nor have many other people as it’s not pegged to any other currency like the euro or dollar, and not accepted anywhere else either; so the dollar rules in Angola, as it does in most of Africa.

Gold carried on as she drove out of the airport onto the main road to Luanda. 'Erdinger is at the Intercontinental Hotel. He must have pre-booked - he walked in with his men and one of the front desk people immediately passed over a key, suite 7.'

'You've got good eyes.' I was impressed.

'I checked the number on the empty hook as I booked in.'

'How much?'

'His suite is six hundred and fifty, my room a hundred and forty.'

'Kwanzas?' No chance.

She laughed. 'Dollars.'

'With breakfast, I hope.'

'Yes, breakfast included. Look at this.'

She pulled up a picture on her mobile. It was an A board stood in the hotel foyer. I didn't understand the language, but I did recognise the triangle motif of Pyramid.

I shrugged. 'I don't read Angolan.'

'It's Portuguese, that's the official language here – ex-Brazilian colony. Most people speak English as well.'

'You speak Portuguese?

'A little, enough to understand this.'

She never ceases to surprise me. ‘So what does it say?’

‘There’s a meeting the day after tomorrow at eleven in the morning in one of the large meeting rooms for delegates to the ‘Pyramide’ conference.’

‘Pyramide?’

‘Yes that’s the German translation.’

I took a deep breath and smiled. ‘We could wipe the whole lot out in one go.’

‘How did I know you’d say that? Come on, let’s find you a room for the night – got to be a homeless shelter somewhere around.’

Cheeky bitch.

CHAPTER 10

I booked into a cheap motel half a mile from the Intercontinental, took a shower, bought a cheap razor from reception, shaved, and was about to take forty winks when Woodward rang.

'British Equestrian Society, Donkey Rides Division – would you like to book a ride?'

He ignored it. 'Your box is at the Embassy. What passport are you using?'

'Lakenheath.'

'I'll text them to expect you.'

Click, and he was gone.

I looked up the Embassy on my mobile; it was on the way, between the motel and the Intercontinental. That was good, I would feel much better with a PKK in my jacket pocket. I wandered out and along the busy street, paid a dollar for a pair of sunglasses and called Gold. I tried her on the comms but it only has about a hundred metre range, so no go. I used my mobile.

'Yes?'

She's a lady of few words.

'The box is at the Embassy, I'm going to pick it up on my way to you.'

'Okay, but don't come here – the place is crawling with security. I'll come to the motel.'

I picked up the box without any fuss and got back to the motel as Gold's Suzuki drove in and stopped on the parking lot outside the row of rooms. We sorted out the box, took a gun and ammunition each, and the rest went into the Burberry. I felt a lot better now; a tradesman can't work without the tools of his trade, eh?

Now it was time to watch and wait. In this business you never go in blind – you need to know all there is about your enemy and their location.

We went to the Hotel and settled in the bar. The security seemed to have settled down; maybe all the Pyramid delegates had arrived and were safely in their rooms. Nevertheless it was busy with holiday makers and business types, which was good. We took separate seats well apart from each other; if somebody recognised me I didn't want them to suss Gold was with me. Suite 7's key was not on the hook, so Erdinger was in.

But not for long. We had hardly sat down when he and one of his two shadows came out of a lift. He left his key at the reception desk and walked outside where the doorman hailed them a taxi. We could have taken another one and done the 'follow that car' routine, but in places like Angola, with a recent history of civil war and army coups, half the working population are paid for any tip-offs to the security forces about foreigners behaving suspiciously, so best not to take a chance. I walked over to the lifts and Gold followed.

'What floor is his suite?'

'Six.'

The lift was crammed. I looked around, trying to see if anybody looked like the opposition. Not really; a couple of businessmen, one with an attaché case, and the rest were family holiday makers chatting continually in a language I didn't understand.

The man with the attaché case got out with us on Floor Six. We walked along the corridor behind him checking the suite numbers. He stopped outside suite 7. I couldn't believe our luck. I nodded to Gold, who knew just what I was thinking. She walked on a little way as I knelt down out of sight of the Suite 7 security peephole and pretended to tie my shoe lace. If the man had looked, he would have seen my shoes were Velcro fastened. I took my PKK from my pocket and clicked the safety off.

The door opened and a goon nodded and motioned the man to enter no words were spoken between the two. As the man stepped inside, I launched myself up and into his back, which sent him forward into the goon and both crashed onto the floor of the suite. The goon's pistol fell from his hand and bounced away across the carpet; he tried to scramble to his feet, but the handle of my gun hitting the back of his head with force put his lights out and he slumped to the floor. I heard a grunt behind me and turned as Gold took care of the man with the attaché case who was also struggling to his knees. She took hold of his shirt collar and pulled him one way and then the other, ramming his head into the concrete wall, and out he went as well. The attaché case was fastened to him by a chain padlocked to a wrist bracelet.

'I hope he has the key, or I might have to amputate,' I said, holding up his arm.

He did have the key; it was in his pocket with another one. I freed the case from the chain and tried the second key on the attaché case clasp. It opened to reveal a small box, the type you would expect to find in a jeweller's with a necklace spread inside. No necklace in this one – just a double row of diamonds, not one smaller than your little fingernail.

'Oh wow!' Gold was impressed, which is unusual for her.

I closed the case and put it in the Burberry. ‘Right, a quick search – anything with the Pyramid symbol on it we photograph.’

It took just a few minutes to do the search; there was only one writing desk in the suite, and that was where we found three folders with the symbol on their covers. They were all in German, so I had no idea what they were about. I used the camera option on Woodward’s mobile to work my way through the pages of each one. I’d send them to him later.

‘Time to go,’ I said as I took a picture of the last one and then replaced the folders in the desk. We didn’t know how long Erdinger would be, and if he wasn’t already aware I was here in Luanda then I certainly didn’t want to alert him. The only way he could get to know about my presence was from the goon on the floor, who would be able to identify me if they had a mugshot of me. So he had to go. And go he did. I dragged him onto the balcony, and he went head-first over the glass wall. Next stop for him would be the pavement. That would create a panic outside the hotel and I could slip away. Gold would go to her room, and once things had quietened down sit in the bar with a book and watch for Erdinger in case he decided to move out. I guessed that when he returned he would either find the man with an empty attaché case still in his room, or the man would recover enough before Erdinger returned to sound the alarm. Whichever way round it was, the obvious conclusion was that there had been a robbery.

'Right, job done – let's go,' I said, checking the man was still out cold and not feigning it by giving him a hefty kick in the ribs. No reaction, he was still out. He hadn't seen my face, so he could live.

We made our way to the lift, passing a couple in the corridor who took no notice of us. The lift was still open at the floor and we had it to ourselves. Once inside, I held out my hand to Gold. Reluctantly she pulled the diamond case from the Burberry and passed it over.

'All bonuses are shared equally,' I said.

'But diamonds are a girl's best friend,' she argued, raising her eyebrows.

'And I'm a diamond geezer,' I said, putting it in my pocket.

Gold left the lift at her floor and I travelled on down to the ground floor. I arranged to come back and meet her in the hotel bar later to get pictures of any of the Pyramid delegates booking in that |I could send to Woodward. The foyer was in a state of pandemonium, with staff and customers gathered at the door looking out whilst the people on the street were looking up and pointing at the hotel balconies. The goon had landed on a taxi, and the driver was not a happy man; he wasn't going to get a fare with a body draped over the bent roof. The police had arrived, and as I slipped past the back of the throng an ambulance pulled up with its sirens screaming at a million decibels.

Back in the motel room I checked that I hadn't had any visitors. Easy to do – I just leave a drawer open a centimetre; if anybody had taken a look they'd automatically close it flush afterwards. Nobody had. I sent the folder pictures to Woodward, popped along the street and bought a light blue summer jacket. I wasn't going to wear the fawn one from earlier just in case hotel CCTV had picked us out. I guessed Gold would do the same; it is standard procedure after a job.

She had. She joined me in the bar dressed in a dark green trouser suit with the Burberry on her shoulder. Looking around at the other people cramming the bar, I would think that whoever imports Hawaiian shirts and skirts into Luanda must be making a fortune. I hoped we didn't stand out for being dressed too dull!

I had taken a small table with a view of the Reception desk and noticed that the A board advertising the Pyramid Conference was now standing on the desk beside one of the check-in computers.

It was quite a while before anybody used that check-in, and then about nine o'clock it suddenly got very busy.

'Looks like a coach has arrived,' I said to Gold.

She was busy on her mobile. 'It has, from the airport. Six planes landed in the last hour, all from Eastern Europe.'

I used Woodward's phone to get pictures of all the arrivals checking in at the Pyramid desk.

'We need to get inside their meeting room,' I said.

Gold smiled a knowing smile. 'Leave a welcome present?'

'Yes, we have an early start tomorrow. Order a room service breakfast for seven o'clock.'

She didn't ask why; she knew I had a plan.

CHAPTER 11

I went back to my motel; nobody had been in my room. I sent Woodward the delegate pictures, set my watch alarm to six in the morning and went to bed. I slept well, woke before the alarm did, showered and strolled to the Intercontinental. The aroma of a full English breakfast filled the bar area which was now the breakfast room, and beginning to fill up with hungry guests queuing with their plates at the self service area. Tempting, but I had a job to do.

I took the stairs to Gold's floor. She was dressed and ready to go. She passed me a PKK and a box of a hundred bullets from the Burberry and settled down to wait for her breakfast.

Dead on seven o'clock came a knock on the door. I hid against the wall on the side that would be hidden when the door opened. Gold stood at the far side of the room by the window table, her back to the door, pretending to be busy with something.

She shouted, 'Come in.'

The middle-aged porter entered with a tray and waited instructions.

'Gold waved a hand towards the telephone desk. 'On there, please.'

The porter walked over and placed the tray down and lifted the large metal dome cover as Gold reached into her pocket and took out some dollar bills, which drew his attention away from me coming up behind and cracking the pistol handle against the back of his head. He went out like a light and crumpled to the floor. I closed the room door quickly. I was glad the room service had been a man; if it had been a female then Gold would have had to do the next bit. I wouldn't like that – she is my back-up, she watches my back, and having her around gives me peace of mind when I'm working. I don't think she would have the same peace of mind if the roles were reversed.

I changed into the porter's jacket, waistcoat and trousers. They were a bit large, but that was better than too small. Gold ripped the telephone wire from the wall and tied the porter's hands behind him, before propping him up against the bed and running the wire round a bed post and fastening him to it. She fetched a new flannel from the bathroom, took it out of its bag and stuffed it in his mouth. If he did wake up he wasn't going anywhere quickly. I cleared the breakfast tray, took a sneaky bite from a sausage, and Gold passed me the Semtex sticks and fuses from the Burberry, which I covered with the tray's metal heat dome.

'Dinner is served.' She laughed as she folded my clothes and put them on top of the flash grenades and smoke bombs in the Burberry, which she slung over her shoulder. 'Okay, you go first and I'll follow.'

I checked the corridor; a few holidaymakers were either going to or coming back from breakfast and sauntering along. I wasn't worried about them, it was staff I was looking for; in my porter's clothes I had to avoid them. All clear, so I made my way to the stairs at the end of the corridor and started down. Foreign voices and laughter came up the stairwell below, I carefully looked over and down. Shit! Two uniformed staff were on their way up. I retraced my steps to the corridor and stepped into the lift just as the doors closed. I smiled to the other five occupants; one was Gold. She would have realised what had happened. We didn't speak.

At the ground floor I stood back and let the others out with a smile and a slight bow. All smiled back except Gold, who was last to leave and poked her tongue out. I left the lift, keeping my head inclined downwards, and skirted the large reception foyer which was now busy with the residents going to and from breakfast and those leaving the hotel wheeling their suitcases to the doors. Outside, coaches to the airport were lined up for them. I turned left off the foyer down a plush carpeted empty corridor to the various meeting rooms. The Pyramid one was sign posted with another A board. I looked through the glass window in the double entry doors; it was empty. It was also open, so I went inside. In the centre a very big and wide oblong boardroom table that had twenty-four seats placed around it. Each one with its own choice of two bottles of spring water, a glass and a cloth serviette folded into a peak. What I took to be Erdinger's chair was plusher than the rest, and his place detached from the rest at the head of the table.

It was time to go to work. I crawled under the table with the breakfast tray and lifted the dome off. I checked my watch; it was just past eight. The Pyramid meeting was at eleven, so let them get settled and then bang. I started each of the digital detonators at 8 a.m. and set them to explode at 11.30 a.m. Their small explosions would set off the large explosion of the Semtex I pushed their plugs into. Each stick of Semtex has a pull-off strip – pull it off and an adhesive strip along the Semtex is exposed, which you press against whatever it is you want blown up and there it stays until it detonates. Armament manufacturers make things so much easier these days. Not so long ago you would have to Sellotape the detonator to the Semtex and then somehow fasten the Semtex to the item to be destroyed. Awkward, and time consuming. I moved around under the table, sticking the Semtex sticks about six feet from the edge at regular intervals. One I kept back; that one was destined for the underside of Erdinger's chair.

I finished placing and priming the other five when the doors opened and I could see two pairs of legs and trolley wheels. The trolley went round the table, stopping for a moment behind each chair, and the movement of the legs showed one person pushing it and the other taking something off it and placing it on the table in front of the chairs. Probably the meeting agenda. I smiled to myself. I bet the final page doesn't say *get blown up* under any other business.

My heart stopped and I reached for my gun. One of the fools had dropped a folder and papers had spilled from it onto the floor; if he looked this way as he picked them up, he would see me. He didn't; he sank to his knees facing away from the table and scooped them up before standing again. The trolley continued around the table, and then it and the two men left. I crawled under the table to the top chair and, reaching underneath the seat, stuck the remaining Semtex stick and detonator against it. This conference was going to have an explosive ending! I crawled out and stood up; the ache in my lower back was a polite way of my body telling me it was probably getting too old for this kind of work, and maybe it was time to think about retiring to a Caribbean island. Trouble was I was *persona non gratis* in most of them. I carried the tray and walked to the double doors, and looked back to make sure I hadn't left anything behind. Looking back was a mistake. As I looked back, two goons looked in through the glass and saw me before I saw them. I walked out and there they were, one either side of the doors, and both with their pistols aimed at me. If I'd gone for my gun I would have been dead before I pulled it from my pocket. One spoke to me; I didn't understand the language, so he waved a hand to indicate I lift the tray dome. I did so – maybe he was expecting a breakfast and that I really was a room service porter? No chance. Goon Two took the tray and dome from me and put it down on the floor and patted me down; room service doesn't usually have a gun in their pocket, and he gave an excited string of words as he found it and pulled it out. I guess he said that I had better be taken to Erdinger right away, as they gave me a push in the back towards the far end of the corridor where the staff lifts were, well away from the foyer. We took one up to the sixth floor and Erdinger's suite. I was expecting some kind of beating on the way which might have given me a chance to turn the tables, but no, nothing nasty. Perhaps the painful interrogation would come with Erdinger asking the questions?

CHAPTER 12

He wasn't in the suite, it was empty. I was motioned to sit on a chair as they both sat on the plush low sofa pointing their pistols at me. Perhaps the goons didn't know about the London killings? Perhaps they thought I really might be room service staff? If Erdinger recognised me as his son's assassin, perhaps I'd be going over the balcony? I just hoped that Gold was aware of my situation and was around.

A loud knock at the door interrupted my thoughts, and the goons' conversation. One of them went to the door and raised the peephole cover and looked through. The .45 bullet that came through it from the outside shattered the magnifying glass, passed through his right eye and bounced around the inside of his skull before settling somewhere in his brain as he fell to the floor.

I didn't need a second chance; the second goon was struggling to get up off the low sofa when my foot hit his throat and sent him sprawling back with a broken trachea – that's the windpipe to those not in the medical profession. His body writhed on the sofa and he clutched his neck, coughing and spluttering as the air in his lungs gave out. I picked up my gun from the desk they had left it on and put him out of his pain with one bullet between the eyes. I opened the door and Gold stepped in.

'Room service, sir?'

Cheeky sod. I shut the door behind her and slipped the security chain across. We had two bodies to get rid of; they needed to be hidden, and not found before the 11.30 a.m. firework display. Oh for a pair of Luandan magicians, eh?

We thought about it. We couldn't leave them in the room, so Gold suggested the Room Service closet. Each floor had one, a small room for keeping fresh linen and cleaning materials. She went out to find it and came back smiling.

'It's halfway along the corridor, no lock – and guess what?'

I really didn't feel the time was right for twenty questions.

'What?'

'Laundry baskets, nice big wicker laundry baskets on wheels. Off you go.'

I got the picture; nobody would question the room service man pushing a laundry basket. I hurried down the corridor and she was right – two large mobile baskets full of linen ready to be cleaned were parked at the back of the closet. I pulled half the linen out of one; there had to be room for two bodies, I didn't want to make a second journey, and besides that, time was marching on. I pushed it along the corridor and into the suite.

We wrapped each goon in a duvet and then put them at the bottom of the basket with the rest of the laundry piled on top. It looked good. She gave me my clothes from the Burberry which I put on top and she went off to take the lift down to go and bring the car from the car park to the front.

Pushing a heavy mobile laundry basket along a plush carpeted corridor is a bit like walking through deep mud. I struggled with it, but made it without incident and pushed it behind the other basket at the back of the closet. I closed the door, took off the room service man's jacket and trousers and put my own back on before slipping out of the closet and joining three residents at the lift to the ground floor. I noticed a few suited delegates winding their way into the meeting room corridor. I checked my watch: 10.45 a.m.

There were enough Suzuki Jimnys at the front of the hotel to start a used car dealership! Certainly is the most popular car in Angola. I spied Gold's and jumped in.

'Where to?'

‘Anything left in your room?’ I asked, clicking on the seat belt.

‘No, all clear. The box from the Embassy in is in the back with the goodies from the Burberry. You need to put your gun and unused ammo in it.’

I had not given a thought to getting our guns out of the country. She had. Would not have been a good idea to set the airport metal detectors off with a PKK 47, would it? I took mine out of my pocket, knelt up on the seat, reached over to the box and dropped it in, together with the diamond case, as she moved the car out of the hotel car park and onto the road..

‘Right, let’s get to the Embassy and then the airport and get out of here, before the balloon goes up.’

The security chief at the Embassy is a man of few words. In fact, none. I passed the box over to him at the Embassy reception.

‘Would you mind taping this up and addressing it to Mr Woodward at 85 Albert Embankment, London, and popping it in the diplomatic bag? I’m afraid I’m in a bit of a hurry and haven’t had time to buy any tape.’

He smiled, nodded and took it. I do like people who don’t ask questions. He was probably a retired SAS man. But I would, of course, check the number of diamonds once back in London. Well, you never can tell, can you?

We didn't go to my motel, no point; I had paid for a week so nobody would be going into the room for another three days, and even then all they would find is a used razor. Gold drove nice and steady the four and a half miles to the airport – last thing we needed was a police stop for speeding. As we left the main part of the city, police cars and ambulances passed us going the other way, their sirens screaming urgency. I checked my watch, 11.35a.m., and showed it to Gold.

'Must be something big going down in the city?' Gold remarked.

'I can't think what,' I replied as we exchanged a smile.

CHAPTER 13

Things went smoothly at the airport. The man at the car rental didn't stop saying '*thank you thank you*' when Gold returned it three days early and waved away a refund. It would have been in kwanzas and worth about ten pounds sterling at the exchange bureau. We bought separate tickets on an Air France plane that was about to board and joined the queue. Customs was quick; I noticed Gold's Burberry getting a cursory glance inside, but other than carrying my old jacket it was now empty.

I felt like running across the tarmac to the boarding stairs and up to the aircraft door, but ambled in a line with the other passengers a few behind Gold. We climbed the stairs and entered the plane. The tickets weren't numbered and the plane not full, so we sat in a pair of seats as far to the back as we could. Gold took the window seat, I had the gangway, which was okay as I could stretch at least one leg.

The last passenger came aboard, the door was shut, and the stewardess gave the usual visual ritual of where the escape doors were and how to use the oxygen mask. I glanced over at Gold and out of the window to where the runway truck had latched onto the boarding stairs and was pulling them away. I sat back; I felt good. I could relax now. I shut my eyes.

They didn't stay shut for long. Gold nudged me hard with her elbow and pointed out of the window. I leant across and looked out. The boarding stairs were being brought back against the plane. Inside there was activity at the far end of the passenger aisle where stewards were opening the door; they seemed to be in a bit of a panic. From the terminal a group of men walked at pace to the plane. At the foot of the boarding stairs they stopped, shook hands, and just one mounted the steps. How the hell had Alaric Erdinger survived the meeting room explosion?

He took a seat at the front end and we were on our way. I wasn't that concerned as he wouldn't know which alias I was using, and although he might well know who I was, which was very likely as the two goons in the Borough car park knew who they were after – me. But with a bit of luck he wouldn't have seen a mugshot himself.

The flight was uneventful. Erdinger spent most of the flight reading papers from his briefcase and sleeping. When we landed at Heathrow he didn't get any special treatment and went through the green Customs channel in front of me like most of the other passengers. Inside the terminal building Gold went missing; not literally, she was somewhere around keeping an eye on me in case anybody came out of the woodwork to follow me as I followed Erdinger. We were in contact, having assembled our comms and checked they were working in the baggage handling hall. Erdinger's Burgundy Range Rover was waiting at the pick-up point, shining under the terminal lights that pierced the evening's gloom. I clicked my mic and told Gold as he got in and was whisked away.

'His car is here, and he's off.'

'Not a problem, the tracker is still operating so we can keep tabs on him.'

We went separately to the multi-storey car park, paid the charges by card and drove out.

'Which way?' I asked on the comms as I headed out of the airport towards the M4.

'London.'

CHAPTER 14

The tracker put the Range Rover back in its London garage after a quick stop at the Angolan Embassy to let Erdinger off; seemed he was kipping there for the night. No point in hanging around, so I arranged to meet Gold late the next morning. I was looking forward to my own bed; the Luandan motel one was basically a board with a duvet.

I didn't set my alarm, but any thought of a lie-in was knocked on the head with Woodward's mobile buzzing at 8.30 a.m.

I slung my legs out of bed and answered it. 'Where have you been? Your mother's been out looking for you all night.'

He ignored it. 'Have you seen Sky News?'

'No, you woke me.'

'Apparently there was a coup attempt in Angola yesterday. Visiting dignitaries blown up in a hotel.'

'Dear oh dear, tut tut – how dreadful,' I said without emotion rubbing the sleep from my eyes and still only half awake.

'Two of our MPs were killed.'

'What?' Now I was fully awake.

‘Robert Munroe and Clive Jacobs, both members of the Foreign Affairs Select Committee who were on a fact-finding mission.’

‘Dead?’

‘Yes, but it seems you missed the primary target. Border Force tell me he flew back into the UK last night.’

‘I know, we were on the same plane.’

‘Right, we had better have a chat at that awful Concourse café. We will be there at midday, so don’t be late.’

Click, and he was gone. *‘We will be there at midday...’* We? Was he bringing somebody? I picked up my remote and clicked on Sky News. The Semtex had made a right mess of the hotel meeting room and the others around it. The reporter said the terrorist movement FLEC, a separatist movement from the oil rich northern part of the country, was thought to be responsible, and warrants had been issued for the arrest of their leaders. The reporter continued by giving the names and occupations of those killed as their photos rolled through. I sort of recognised Munroe and Jacobs, as you do with celebrity mugshots, but they didn’t ring any bells. With an over-bloated six hundred and thirty-five MPs with their snouts in the trough in the Commons, two wouldn’t be missed. The rest of the dead were mainly Eastern European big business owners, or politicians from their country of origin. I did recognise some of them. Christ, the Pyramid had some big hitters supporting it! Trouble was, the biggest hitter was still out there.

I had my usual breakfast, bran flakes with raisins and walnuts, took a shower, dressed casual but smart, and gave Gold a call at about ten.

'You up?'

'For the last three hours. I take it you watched the news?'

'Yes.'

'Seems we did some damage in Angola.'

'Probably started an internal war between the government and the rebels. Woodward's been on – two of the dead were MPs.'

There was a short silence. 'Our MPs?'

'Yes.'

'That makes sense.'

Not to me it didn't. 'What do you mean?'

'I'm parked along the side of Parliament Square – the tracker went off at 7.30 a.m. and showed Erdinger's car leaving the garage and stopping for a short time at the Embassy before coming to Westminster. It is in the MPs' underground car park.'

'What, the one *inside* the Palace of Westminster?'

'That very one.'

'Well, well, well, our man seems to have important friends in high places. Woodward wants a meet at the Concourse at midday.'

'Okay, you want me to shadow you or stay here and keep with Erdinger?'

I thought for a moment. Woodward would have his protection chaps with him, so I should be covered. 'No, you stay with Erdinger. I'll ring you when Woodward arrives and I'll leave the line open.'

'Okay.'

I rang Woodward and told him of Erdinger's visit to the seat of democracy. He didn't sound surprised. My box of goodies had arrived from Luanda and he would bring it to the concourse; that was quick. I took off my jacket, slipped on my shoulder holster and buttoned it up. I would feel much better when it was holding my PPK.

CHAPTER 15

'Coffee?'

'Please.'

The lady behind the counter at the Charing Cross Station concourse cafe managed a brief smile as the machine spat, hissed and dribbled me out a coffee. Three pounds twenty! Christ, my bag of French Style ground beans from Morrisons didn't cost that and gave me a week's coffees! I took it to a table at the front where I could see the whole of the concourse. I was five minutes early. I'd found a space in Northumberland Street to park Annie's rental and walked the rest of the way, taking a detour round the fountains in Trafalgar Square in case I had a tail; I hadn't. I gave Gold a call, and she told me Erdinger's car had not emerged from Parliament as yet. I left the line open and placed my phone on the table. Dead on midday, Woodward strode across the concourse with his fawn Crombie flapping behind, my box of tricks from Angola under his arm and his two protection officers following at a discreet distance.

He acknowledged me with a curt, 'Nevis', and placed my box on an empty chair beside me. 'I believe this is yours.' He then enacted his usual flapping at a chair seat with his leather gloves to remove any biscuit crumbs or other cafe detritus waiting to soil his coat when he sat down. I didn't offer him a coffee, as the offer would only have been met with a libellous insult of British Rail's catering abilities.

'Good afternoon, Ben,' said another voice from behind me, a voice I recognised.

Commander Dick Clancy shook my hand and took a seat without all the Woodward glove-flapping. It was all falling into place now. I had wondered at the time of the Borough High Street car park episode why Clancy had arrived on the scene. I was about to find out.

Woodward flapped a hand towards Clancy. 'You know Commander Clancy, Organised Crime.' It was a statement; he obviously knew that I had previous with Clancy.

I nodded, and Woodward continued. 'I'll let the Commander explain his interest in Erdinger.' He opened his hand to Clancy, giving him the floor.

Clancy took the reins. 'For some time now, Ben, my department has been working with Counter Terrorism to find how and where the major drug gangs in the UK, especially London, managed to import large amounts of fentanyl pills into the country that we couldn't find a route for. As you know, fentanyl is an opioid one hundred times more addictive than heroin, and kills tens of thousands of Americans every year, and the Home Office is adamant that we don't allow it to get a foothold here. The pills weren't coming in by the usual means of mules a few kilos at a time as the quantities hitting the streets were too large, and despite Border Force doing additional stops and searches at the ports and harbours we drew blanks. The only clue we had was the fentanyl pills themselves.' He took a small envelope from his coat pocket and shook out two tablets, and pushed one across the table to me. I didn't need a second look; the pill had a pyramid engraved as a 'trademark'.

I looked from Woodward to Clancy. 'Erdinger's pyramid.'

They both nodded. 'Yes, the Pyramid,' continued Clancy. 'At first it didn't mean a thing to us or Terrorism Command. Most of the cartels producing these pills and kilos of heroin have a trademark, but this was a new one, so we quietly circulated it around the various task forces and intelligence units.'

'Including MI6,' Woodward interjected.

'Who pointed us towards Erdinger and his Pyramid group,' Clancy continued. 'So we turned our attention to them with some surprising results. Erdinger has some very influential friends. He is at this very moment inside Parliament meeting with Sir Henry Talbot, head of the Commons Select Committee on Foreign Affairs. Both Munroe and Jacobs were members of that committee and went on many fact-finding missions abroad. Once we established the relationship between Erdinger and this committee, we then backtracked and found that the amount of fentanyl pills on the London streets increased substantially after Munroe and Jacobs returned from one of their trips. Because they would be carrying Government papers relating to their observations of the country they had visited, they had use of the diplomatic bag protocol for their luggage – straight through Customs, no searches. No doubt their suitcases went out full of clothes, but they came back full of pills – pills sold on to the UK drug lords for a hefty profit of millions of pounds that financed the Pyramid group in the UK. No doubt the same or similar route is used in the other countries they are building a presence in.'

Woodward took over. 'Our chaps in the Luanda Embassy have cleared Munroe and Jacobs's hotel rooms since the explosion and confirmed the contents of their suitcases to be pills. The cases were sent back under diplomatic immunity and are in the Embassy.

‘So the delegates at the Luanda conference were just a bunch of couriers, not genuine businessmen and politicians?’

Woodward nodded. ‘Quite, their publicly perceived occupations were just a cover for their Pyramid activities. Pyramid money would have been used in bribes and assassinations to elevate them to their high business or political positions.’

‘Erdinger is going to be really pissed off with me, isn’t he.’

Woodward shrugged. ‘If he knows it was you, yes.’

‘Well, he knew it was me that shot his son in Montenegro, or why did he send two goons to kill me? The thing is, how did he know it was me?’

Woodward nodded. ‘Yes, there is that. I am afraid I have to conclude that we seem to have a problem with the plumbing at our organisation. I’m working on it.’

A *problem with the plumbing* is an MI6 term for a leak. Somebody in Woodward’s team was working for Erdinger. I wasn’t quite sure what this meeting was for. Did I still take out Erdinger? Why all this information?

I posed the question. ‘So, what’s the plan, and how do I fit in, if I fit in?’

Clancy smiled and Woodward laughed.

‘Oh, you fit in, Nevis. The Pyramid is like all criminal organisations – if you cut off the head, the tail dies.’

‘The head being Erdinger,’ I said.

Woodward nodded. ‘Yes.’

‘However,’ Clancy held up a finger, ‘My department can’t be part of that. The Met does not take out people or facilitate any opportunities for that sort of operation. But, being that we are aware of the security forces’ interest in this operation, we have to express an interest as we are looking at the drug dealing side of it. Our interest would be to get enough solid evidence of Henry Talbot’s involvement in drug dealing to be able to arrest him. And that is the full extent of our interest.’ He paused before adding, ‘Officially.’

‘And if Talbot was to meet with a fatal accident?’ Woodward asked.

‘It would save my department a lot of time and money.’ Clancy smiled at me. The inference was clear; he too wanted Talbot dead. He stood up and pulled out a lanyard neck strap with a security clearance ID pass attached to the end of it from his pocket and passed it to me.

‘You might find this useful.’ I took it and looked at it. My mugshot on a Parliamentary Estate Security Pass, Access All Areas, name DCI John Smith. Detective Chief Inspector. That should impress the gate police. Clancy squeezed my shoulder. Not often I get a show of affection from him; usually it’s cold indifference. ‘Well, I have to go. Good to see you, Ben – take care.’ Woodward stood, they shook hands, and Clancy left.

Woodward stayed standing. ‘Your mission is still active, Nevis. I want Erdinger out of the picture and the Pyramid operation in the UK demolished now, before it gains any traction. Don’t leave that behind.’ He nodded to the box on the seat, gave me a perfunctory nod, and swept out of the cafe with his protection duo in his wake.

‘Well, did you get all that?’ I picked up my mobile and spoke.

‘Most of it’, Gold replied. ‘And I have some news for you,’

‘Go on.’

‘Sir Henry Talbot is a client of mine.’

It took a few seconds for that news to sink in. ‘You are joking?’

‘No.’

Gold doesn’t joke.

'Anyway, to bring you up-to-date, he and Erdinger came out of Parliament together and they have made the quick trip to the Angolan Embassy in Erdinger's car. They're both still inside the Embassy and the car is outside with the chauffeur standing by, so looks like they are not going to be very long.'

Opportunity knocks, and I could hear an opportunity knocking loudly. 'I'll fill you in later, but I've got a Parliamentary Pass courtesy of Organised Crime – the other voice you heard at the cafe was Dick Clancy and he gave it to me, it's in the name of John Smith with my mugshot. If Talbot is with Erdinger then I'm going to try and take a look in his office whilst he's out. Let me know if he or they return to Parliament. I'll put my comms on now.'

'Okay, I'll do the same.'

It takes just a minute or two to put the ear piece in and clip the mic on. Both parts of the comms have lithium batteries giving a two-mile reception, so I reasoned Gold and I would be in contact. I checked when mine were in place; no problem, good reception.

I hurried back to the car in Northumberland Avenue and sat inside to open the goodie box, slipping a magazine into my PKK before pushing it into my shoulder holster.

I left the car where it was and took a black cab to Parliament – a short trip, but no point in wasting time using the car and then taking half an hour finding somewhere to park it at the other end. I had checked the pass, but it didn't give access to the MPs' underground garage. And anyway, the cabbie was happy with a tenner for five minutes work.

I had no problem at the gate, was even called 'sir' after my new pass was checked. Inside I followed the public corridors to the central area where the TV companies have their equipment set up. I've been in a few times before, even done the tour, but I've never found the trough they've all got their snouts in. You're beginning to get the gist of my political leanings, eh, dear reader? I'm slightly to the left of Guy Fawkes. I approached the reception desk. Photos of Munroe and Jacobs were propped up at the end with black mourning cloth draped around them. I flashed my card.

'Henry Talbot is expecting me.'

The desk clerk checked his ledger. 'I am afraid Sir Henry is out, sir.'

'Okay.' I checked my watch. 'I'm a bit early, I'll go up and get a coffee. Is he still in room 264?' It was the first number that came into my head, don't ask why.

The clerk turned a page and ran a finger down a list. 'He's 172, sir.'

I sounded surprised. 'Oh, well it has been a while since I saw him last. Point me in the right direction, please.'

He indicated a corridor to the left. 'Take the corridor and then the stairs or lift to the first floor, sir. 172 is near the far end. The cafe is on the second floor.'

I nodded my appreciation and walked slowly off and into the corridor. Once out of his view I hastened my pace to the stairs. I never use lifts; lifts have CCTV.

MPs usually share three to an office because of the lack of office space in the old building. A couple of hundred of them even have to share their offices in Portcullis House, which is over the other side of the road from Parliament in Bridge Street on the Embankment and built for them. From there they have to go to and fro, through a tunnel under the road.

Being knighted, *Sir* Henry Talbot gets his own office in Parliament, and he doesn't share it, which meant with him away at the Angolan Embassy it should be empty. It was, and the door was unlocked, which told me that he didn't have anything incriminating in the office. The furniture was surprisin , I was expecting old brown wood, but it was modern with a well-padded tubular steel sofa and chairs and a large circular desk. It had a small alcove off one side with a sink, a photocopier, computer and a large screen on the wall showing the chamber. An unlocked steel filing cabinet looked more interesting than it was. Inside were the items for making tea or coffee, some cups and towels. I opened the desk drawer – this was more interesting: manila folders. I shifted through them; Expenses, Commons Programme, Lords Programme, Select Committee Agenda – all boring stuff, except the last one: no name, just a pyramid drawn on the front in felt tip.

'Looks like we are on the move,' said Gold's voice in my ear.

I clicked my mic on. 'Okay, I'm in Talbot's office having a dig around. Let me know if they are coming here.'

'I would think so – he and Erdinger have parted at the Embassy door. Erdinger has gone back inside, and Talbot is in the Range Rover.'

'Alright, when you get here call me.'

'Will do.'

I took the pyramid folder to the photocopier, switched it on and started taking copies of the ten pages inside.

'Henry not here?' A voice behind me asked.

I nearly jumped out of my skin! I hadn't heard the door open over the noise of the copier churning out copies. A man in a rumpled suit stood halfway in the door. He was middle-aged and overweight, so must be an MP. I smiled and shook my head.

'No, he's out for the day.' I flashed my new pass – he was too far away to actually read it. 'Got some trouble with the copier, so I'm giving it a quick service.' Hopefully he would think I was a mechanic.

He did. 'Bloody machines are so old they are always breaking down or clogging up – should have been replaced ages ago. Mine regularly packs up. Usual excuse from finance, no money for replacements.'

I nodded and laughed. *Yes, I thought, spent all the money on subsidised food and wine for you lot.*

And he was gone. I finished the copying, put the folder back in the drawer, and I was gone too.

Gold spoke. 'Talbot's been dropped off and is coming in, he's using the Millbank entrance.'

‘Okay, I’ll go out that way – I want to get a look at him. Pick me up further along Millbank by the park.’

‘Will do.’

I took the stairs two at a time and made my way to the public entrance. If Talbot checked in at the desk, which is not obligatory, he would be told a detective had been asking for him, and that might well raise his concerns.

The public foyer was busy – school parties, WI and PROBUS visits – but Talbot was an easy pick out as he hurried between them. I would put him in his early sixties, quite short really, receding hair line and glasses, with the rotund figure of another MP who had obviously taken advantage of the subsidised canteens,. Why are most of the nasty people in the world short, have you noticed that? I have – Putin, Hitler, Mussolini, Kim Jon Un, Farage. All short.

Gold was parked at the side of the road fifty metres down from the door. I jumped in.

‘Right, first stop Legoland. I have some papers to leave for Woodward to look at.’ I turned and gave Gold a broad smile. ‘And then Northumberland Avenue to pick up my car, and on the way you can tell me all about your, ahem, business dealings with Sir Henry Talbot.' This could be interesting…

CHAPTER 16

The next morning Henry Talbot checked his tie was straight in the mirror in his parliamentary office. ‘Bloody Wednesdays, pain in the backside,’ he muttered to himself. Wednesdays were PMQs, Prime Minister’s Questions in the Commons, and MPs were expected to be in the chamber to whoop and cheer like monkeys at a tea party. MPs of both sides consider it a waste of time; all their respective leaders do is spout the usual guff about how wonderful they are and how well they are doing. If one of them ever actually answered a question, the Speaker of the House would have to call a halt for them to be medically examined.

Talbot made his way down the stairs into the noisy chamber through a lobby door and took his seat on the back row. He checked his watch; he was due at the Angolan Embassy at 1.30 p.m., so hopefully the Speaker would close the proceedings on time at 12.30 p.m.

George Chandler, MP for Nottingham North, slipped into his seat beside Talbot.

‘Good morning, Henry,’

‘Morning, George.’

‘Bloody waste of time, eh?’

Talbot nodded in agreement. 'Isn't it just. I've a mountain of work waiting.'

'Me too.'

Talbot thought about pointing out to Chandler that if the MP for Nottingham North spent less time lounging around in the bars imbibing tax payer-funded whiskey and more time in his office, his workload might diminish somewhat. But he thought better of it.

'Your photocopier okay?'

Talbot wondered about the reason for that question. 'Yes, fine – do you want to use it? Yours on the blink again?'

'No, no. I popped into your office yesterday and the mechanic was working on it, said you'd got a problem.'

Alarm bells rang in Talbot's head. He covered. 'Oh, yes, yes, I'd forgotten about that. All okay now.'

The PM entered the chamber and the monkeys whooped.

****

At the end of PMQs Talbot was the first one out of the Chamber and hurried down the corridor to the security desk.

'Are the photocopy machines being serviced?'

The clerk checked his maintenance diary. ‘No, Sir Henry, not due a service for another month. Have you got trouble with yours Sir? I can send somebody up?’

Talbot thought fast. ‘No, no, I’ve a lot of copying to do and didn’t want to have to stop halfway through. Thank you.’ He took a step away before the clerk remembered.

‘Oh, I nearly forgot, sir – there was a detective looking for you yesterday when you were out. I sent him up to the canteen to wait. Did he find you?’

Talbot’s heart missed a beat, but he thought fast. ‘Yes, yes, thank you – just one of my constituents with a problem with a planning application. Thank you.’

He made his way up to his office and immediately checked the files. All present and correct. He was worried.

CHAPTER 17

Erdinger and the Angolan Ambassador walked Henry Talbot from the Ambassador's office in the Angolan Embassy to the front door where Erdinger's car waited.

They shook hands.

'That was an exceedingly nice gesture, Ambassador,' Talbot said. 'Exceedingly generous, and I'm sure the two families will be very grateful'

'Not at all, Sir Henry – it is the least we can do under such awful circumstances.'

Erdinger held the rear door of the car open for Talbot to get in. 'I'll catch up with you later, Sir Henry – and don't worry about that detective paying a visit yesterday, probably some parking ticket you haven't paid. I'll call you later.'

Talbot wasn't pacified; detectives don't chase unpaid parking fines.

Erdinger shut the door and the car pulled away. The meeting had gone exactly as he had planned it. He patted the Ambassador on the shoulder and they turned back into the Embassy foyer as a dark blue Kia left its parking spot and slipped into the traffic queue behind the Range Rover and drove past, the sort of car that wouldn't raise any eyebrows in that part of London.

Back in the Ambassador's office Erdinger took a seat opposite the Ambassador at the palatial desk in his office. The Angolan Embassy doesn't look much from the front, but it extends at the back into quite a large property.

'Well, that's the personal bit sorted for the families – what about the official line, what's happening there?' the Ambassador asked.

Alaric Erdinger gave a dismissive shrug. 'All clear – the Home Office has gone along with your Government's assessment that it was FLEC. Talbot will be rushing off now to get an interview on the six o'clock news channels and denounce them as terrorists, and then he will say how he has met with you in his position as Chair of the Foreign Affairs Select Committee and negotiated the repatriation of the two MPs and pensions from Angola for the two widows, and what a masterful politician he is. He will be, as the English say, as happy as a bunny – on the flip side, of course, he will owe you a favour when the time comes to call one in.'

'Good.' The Angolan Ambassador laughed and relaxed in his padded chair. 'And the diamonds stolen at the hotel?'

Erdinger smiled. 'Don't worry, I told the Luandan police it was a private investment deal – some local criminal gang must have followed the courier to my suite and thought he would be an easy victim to rob. They were then surprised by my guard, shot him and tossed him over the balcony to create a diversion whilst they got away. They actually saved my life.'

'Saved your life?'

'I was made late to the conference – the local police were interviewing me when the bomb went off, otherwise I wouldn't be here now. Fate moves in many ways.' He became serious. 'Those diamonds will have to be replaced, my dealer is waiting for them with the cash – seven million. That cash is to pay the cartel for the pills, the pills that were destroyed in the explosion. It is a loss, but it is also a debt – a debt that has to be paid. You don't cross the cartel, or my dealer.'

'They should be grateful for your business over the years.'

Erdinger laughed. 'And so should your blood diamond traffickers. Do you think they would like not to be paid?'

'I take your point. We have no need to worry about them – the diamonds were laundered through registered companies, insurance will pay for their loss. I'll get another batch sent through as soon as I can. Any more on your son's killing?'

Erdinger shrugged. 'Nothing definite. My people checked the hotels and Customs and found one person of interest – he paid his hotel for a week in advance in cash and disappeared after three days. He flew out of Croatia late on the day my son was shot, but there's no record of him at the border Customs.'

'Name?'

'Henry Portman, it will be an alias. My man in MI6 says they wouldn't use in-house staff on an EU assassination, and gave us three private individuals to check. The only one whose whereabouts we couldn't account for on the day of the shooting was Portman. CCTV at the hotel provided a photo, and my MI6 man put a name to it, Ben Nevis.'

'Could be a coincidence.'

Erdinger laughed. 'No, Nevis masquerades as a private eye specialising in domestic cases, he has an office in The Borough High Street. We sent two men to follow him, two men who ended up dead in an underground car park. Coincidence? He was then spotted near a CBI dinner at the Guildhall that I was attending, and the two men sent to follow him there haven't been seen since – another coincidence? Their car was towed away by the City of London police after six days on double yellow lines.'

'So MI6 are onto you?'

'They have been watching me for several years – nothing they can do, our business is perfectly legal, and with people like Talbot on board we have support in high places able to stamp on any rumours and accusations as soon as they surface. We are doing well, very well – our organisation is growing, especially in Africa. Just like you, we have people waiting for the right time to launch a coup – won't be long now, the senior military commanders in the countries we are interested in, the ones with the rare minerals, are quietly being offered high places in government after a successful coup, control of various utilities and fifty percent of the cash they generate. Putin used that, and look where he is now – top dog. You need to start rumours amongst your political circle that FLEC is massing troops in the north, get people jittery. My people will fake drone shots of them with heavy artillery – your present government will deny this, but the people won't believe them, and then my people will organise marches against the government and we will strike and strike hard.' He smiled. 'So how does that sound... *Mr President?'*

The ambassador smiled. 'It sounds very good, especially the *Mr President* bit.'

They both laughed.

CHAPTER 18

'Is this what you did for a living?'

'Until you came back into my life, yes. A girl's gotta live.'

'And you're still doing it, tut-tut.'

'Pocket money.'

I laughed.

She had pulled in behind Annie Greggs's Honda in Northumberland Avenue, cut the engine, told me to stay put and fiddled with her mobile before passing it over to me. It was on the video app. The video playing was of Sir Henry Talbot holding a stick duster and dusting the furniture and shelves in what appeared to be his hotel room. I know, you're thinking so what, nothing wrong in that? No, there's not, but Sir Henry is wearing an old fashioned maid's bonnet and nothing else. Sir Henry Talbot is stark bollock naked! Out of the picture I can hear a female voice, Gold's, reprimanding him for missing a bit, and he apologises profusely and bends over as a thin cane whacks his backside. He says 'thank you, miss' and carries on dusting.

'That's the bit I enjoy most,' Gold laughs.

It's dynamite, of course it is; any tabloid would pay big money for that video.

‘Where is that?’ I ask.

‘A room in his hotel suite, he stays there when he’s in London at the House.’

‘I don’t wish to pry into your private means, but how often, and how much?’

‘Usually once a fortnight, and mind your own business.’

‘So when he, or any of your clients, decide to end their arrangement with you and say ‘no more, thank you’, you step in with a video and they make a donation to your pension fund?’

‘A large donation.’

‘And how many ‘Sir Henrys’ have you got in play?’

‘That’s my business too.’

The information channel was closed.

‘I’ll send a copy to your phone.’

‘Okay.’ I wasn’t sure what to do with it, but it was a hook into Talbot that would no doubt be useful at some time, but my main objective was Erdinger.

‘I was thinking about how to eliminate Erdinger. He’s obviously staying at the Angolan Embassy, so if he were to have an accident inside there I don’t think the Embassy would be happy for the police to investigate, do you?’

She could see where this devious private eye was going with that.

'I don't think it would even be reported. When have you in mind?'

'Well, we don't know how long he's staying there – he could fly off to one of his Pyramids at any time, so tonight looks good to me. Unless you are otherwise engaged, 'miss'?' I lifted my eyebrows and smiled at her. We arranged to meet later.

CHAPTER 19

I picked up a chicken korma on the way home and parked two streets away from my apartment block. I knew that if I had taken Annie Greggs's old Honda into the residents' underground car park I would have to endure remarks from the security guys on Reception as I checked in.

'Hard times, Mr Hadlow?'

'Don't park it near the rubbish bins sir, collection day tomorrow.'

And the rest.

The korma went down a treat. I brewed a coffee and sipped it whilst catching up with Sky News. Talbot was the lead story; he stood on the steps of the Foreign Office with a few flunkies around him reading a prepared statement. The Angolan Government had repatriated the bodies of Munro and Jacobs and offered pensions to the two widows.

I hope it will be in pounds and not kwanzas. Anything over ten quid in kwanzas and you'll need a wheelbarrow to fetch it.

Talbot droned on about his determination to find the killer, and how all the resources of the Foreign Office and MI6 would be used to that end in collaboration with the Angolan authorities, and how the world must not stoop to the demands of terrorists. I laughed a sarcastic laugh; this is the man assisting a multi-national terrorist organisation, a man in bed with Erdinger's Pyramid organisation, a man whose ultimate aim is to bring down the democratic government he belongs to and take charge.

I can't wait to see his reaction when Gold's video goes public.

The best thing about takeaway food is there's no washing-up – I hate washing- up. I know, you are thinking one man's washing-up is not exactly a big job. It's not the washing, it's the shit you use to do it; the *washing-up liquid*, the biggest pollutant of rivers other than farmers, and all that chemical crap people put in their dishwashers and washing machines.

I settled back on the sofa, set my watch alarm and dozed off. I had arranged to meet with Gold at midnight in Gloucester Place around the corner from the Embassy.

The alarm woke me. I took a shower, (eco-friendly soap before you say anything) strapped my commando knife inside its leather pouch round my right ankle, and slipped on my bullet-proof vest made from PEUD. This is an organic material whose fibres are so closely entwined a bullet can't get through – amazing, eh? But true. I pulled on my black one-piece overall, slipped into a pair of thick black suede rubber-soled soft boots with Velcro straps, slung on a left shoulder holster and tightened the fit and pulled on a pair of black nitrile gloves, tight but comfy. I was ready. I donned a light long-style black coat, put my coms mic and ear piece in my pocket and left the apartment block by the fire stairs to the car park and walked out the rear entrance, avoiding the CCTV, and made my way to Annie Greggs's car. It was still there. If I'd parked my Range Rover there it wouldn't be. There's a waiting list for top of the range cars in Saudi Arabia; Range Rovers, BMW and Mercedes lead the list. I don't think clapped-out Hondas feature very highly on Saudi Arabia's *must have* toy list.

CHAPTER 20

Gold's Kia was parked a hundred metres down the road from the Embassy as I opened the passenger door, took off my coat and put it on the backseat before getting in. 'The car is still in the garage, so Erdinger is still inside,' she said. 'What's the plan?'

I had been thinking about that. 'We need to get him out of the Embassy, too dangerous to break in and kill him. They'll have Embassy security people, and you can be sure Erdinger's added to his circle of goons after Montenegro and then two killed in the Borough and two missing after Guildhall. He's not stupid, he will know he's a target. I think we have to flush him out and see where he bolts to, and then go for him when he's only got his own people with him'

'How do we get him out?'

I smiled at her and passed over a McDonald's bag. Nobody would take a second look at a person carrying a McDonald's burger bag. Gold opened it and pulled out an incendiary stick. There were six in the bag, plus a red spray paint aerosol. I'd called into Gilbert Charles's shop in St Martin's Lane on the way. He is there twenty-four-seven as he lives above it. I'd given him a call on the way with my order; I needed to pay him for the items he had sent to Luanda in the diplomatic bag, and had decided on the plan to kill Erdinger on the drive over there. Incendiary sticks were part of Gilbert's back room stock, as well as a stack of McDonald's bags. He had no doubt smiled to himself when he saw the Honda pull up and my black clothing.

'Working tonight then, Ben?' Gilberthe said with a laugh as I entered the shop.

He didn't get an answer, just a smile back that said 'yes'.

Gold handed the bag back to me. 'Okay, let's go. You carrying?'

'Yes.' I patted my shoulder holster as she leant over to the back seat and pulled the Burberry through before unzipping it and taking out a PPK, before putting the Burberry back and slipping the gun into her pocket.

'I plan on breaking a window,' I said.

She looked at me. 'What with, a bullet?'

'No, I need a hole big enough to slip an incendiary through. Any ideas?'

'Wait there.' She slipped out of the car and I heard the boot open and close. She climbed back in and passed me a heavy wrench. 'Part of the Kia tool kit, don't ask me what it's for.'

I took it and slipped it up my left sleeve.

We left the car and checked the road both ways; nobody about, so we strolled slowly along the opposite side of the road to the Embassy. I held the McDonald's bag in my hand.

'I think the narrow side road is the best option. Nice and dark,' I said.

'Okay, I'll be around.'

'I won't be long, in and out. Give me five minutes and then call the fire brigade.'

The sooner the brigade got there, the sooner those inside would panic and get Erdinger out. I kept to the shadows along Dorset Street and turned down narrow Clay Street that runs along the side of the Embassy. The Embassy loomed above me, and only when you see the side view do you realise how far back it goes. That was good, I wanted to create havoc as far away from the front as I could. There were plenty of windows I could break and lob incendiaries through. All were covered in security bars which were spaced far enough apart for me to get a hand through, and the glass panes were small which was ideal. They wouldn't make a lot of noise when I broke them like a large pane would.

I checked along the street both ways; nobody was about. I took out the aerosol and sprayed FLEC in large letters half a dozen times along the whitewashed wall of the Embassy as I walked along. Then I retraced my steps back towards Dorset Street, reaching through the security bars of three of the windows and smashing one of the small panes with the Kia wrench before pulling the igniting tape off an incendiary which burst into flame like a Roman candle firework and dropping it through the broken glass into the room. Two of the rooms had long curtain drapes against the inside of the windows, so they should burn well and fast unless they were flame retardant. Fingers crossed they weren't.

I got back to Dorset Street and crossed the road before backing into a dark doorway where I could see the Embassy. Funny how time seems to slow down when you are waiting for something to happen quickly. Seemed to take an age before the internal fire alarm in the Embassy started whining like an ambulance siren picking up speed. That would send any staff on duty rushing to the back rooms. I moved quickly across to the front door, ripped the ignite tape off an incendiary and pushed it through the letterbox. Most Embassies don't have letterboxes, for obvious reasons like some joker might pop an incendiary stick through it. I kept to the dark bits of the pavement where I could and made my way quickly back to Gold's Kia. I slipped into the passenger seat as she slipped into the driver's seat. I hadn't seen her along the road, but I knew she would be somewhere near with me in sight, just in case something went wrong. I smiled at her as I put the aerosol and remaining incendiary sticks into the Burberry.

'Easy peasy lemon squeezy.'

'Job's not finished yet, Ben.' Always the one to bring you back down to earth is Gold. 'Brigade's on its way.'

No sooner had she said that than two fire engines came the wrong way down Dorset Street with everything blaring and blue lights flashing. Two firemen jumped off the first engine and ran to the Embassy front door with hand-held extinguishers, whilst others ran a hose down Clay Street and started smashing the rest of the windows of the rooms that were now well ablaze before turning on the jets of water. The two at the front door called for the 'enforcer', a sixteen kilogram hardened steel hand-held battering ram you've probably seen used by the police on drug raids to smash down the front door, and commonly known as a *bosher*. It did the job in just two swipes at the Embassy door, which swung open and was left hanging half off its hinges. We could see the flames inside the foyer which quickly succumbed to the fire fighter's foam extinguishers. Erdinger, two of his goons and his driver who had been in the back of the foyer made for the door; they ran out half drenched in foam And hurried away towards the garage as police arrived, as did quite a few members of the public. Flash bulbs were going off which meant the press had arrived as well; time for us to vanish. Gold moved the car up the road and pulled up in Gloucester Place, well away from all the hubbub. She took out her mobile and clicked up the tracker app before passing it over to me.

'I wonder where he's going to spend the night now,' she said.

'He's on the move.' The app was flashing, 'Going south, Shaftesbury Avenue towards Piccadilly.'

We followed a fair way behind. From Piccadilly Erdinger's car headed to Trafalgar Square and into Whitehall.

I made a guess. 'He's heading to Parliament, must be meeting Talbot?'

'Not this time of night. More likely Talbot's hotel.'

She was right. We followed the app over Westminster Bridge, turned right into Lambeth

Palace Road, round the Lambeth Bridge roundabout and into the Albert Embankment.

Gold nodded. 'Yes, he's heading for the Crowne Plaza, Talbot's hotel. He must have rung Talbot to book him a room.'

'Cheeky bugger, the National Crime Agency building is just round the corner.'

We both smiled at the irony. The tracker stopped at the Crowne Plaza and I clicked it off. Gold checked the time.

'Eleven o'clock – the hotel bars will be busy, plenty of cover.' She parked in a side street opposite the hotel. 'You'd better put your coat on, or they'll think the Milk Tray Man has arrived.'

Cheeky cow. 'I didn't think you were that old?'

'I've seen the repeats on quiz shows.'

Touché. We screwed on silencers to our PPKs. Gold slipped the Burberry on her shoulder and we got out of the car. Then, after checking our comms were working, Gold made her way in at the front of the Plaza whilst I gave her five minutes before following. It was busy. I made my way into the bar, grabbed a newspaper from a pile on the bar and sat down.

Gold came through on the earpiece. 'Talbot's room is 125 on the seventh floor.

Guests have a smart card for entry so there are no keys on hooks to see who is in and who is out. Erdinger's room is 184 on the ninth.'

'How did you find that out?'

'I'm his daughter visiting.'

'Okay, I'll take a look at the ninth floor. I would think he's more likely to be there getting himself together and finding out what's happening at the Embassy than paying a visit to Talbot.'

'Odds on Talbot's with him.'

'Can I get you a drink, sir?' The voice startled me. It was a waitress.

'No, no, I'm fine, thank you.' I gave her my killer smile. It used to work, but these days it's got a one in five hit rate.

'May I take your coat, sir? It's quite hot in here, I can put it in the cloakroom for you?'

'That's very kind, but I'm waiting for one of your guests to come down and then we are off out.'

She nodded and walked away. I rose to go and take a look at the ninth floor and nearly bumped into Talbot coming into the bar as I walked out; he was in a hurry. I circled the foyer and went back in. He was at the far end, seated at a table with two men. One was facing me who I didn't recognise: mid-thirties in a dark suit, looked like a young businessman. The other was sat facing away from me: casual clothes, no jacket, looked older by his grey hair. I took a seat three tables away and pretended to make a phone call on Woodward's mobile while I took a picture and then sent it.

By the way, the older man was leaning forward towards Talbot and jabbing a finger; he was not a happy bunny. Talbot spread his hands in a gesture of acceptance. One last wag of the finger and Mr Casual rose from his seat and turned to leave. My memory speed dialled back through ten years: Jimmy Hanson, once known as the Tablet King, the main supplier of ecstasy pills in the early noughties. I had done some work for him in my early PI days which we won't go into now. He went down for life for killing a competitor, but he was out now; must be on parole or licence.

It all clicked into shape in my head. The fentanyl tablets were for him, he was back in the game. And knowing how Hanson operated, there wasn't room for anybody else. I bent and tied my non-existent shoe lace as he walked past. Talbot and his suited friend were deep in conversation. Talbot looked worried; if he'd taken a wad of cash off Hanson for the pills destroyed in Angola and now couldn't deliver them, he was right to be worried. From memory, the last people that crossed Hanson like that ended up dead in a Range Rover in an Essex wood. I followed Hanson out of the bar; he was on his phone. He left the hotel and got into a BMW that pulled up outside and was driven away. Woodward's phone buzzed in my pocket.

'Emergency Escorts – blonde, brunette or redhead, sir?'

He ignored it. 'The man with Talbot is Justin Parker, Senior Administrator in the Analysis Department. Responsible for analysing the reports that come in from our agents. I think you have pinpointed our leak, Nevis – well done.'

'Is he added to my target list?'

'No, not yet – that would panic the Pyramid people. Leave him be, I can always use him to send false information to Erdinger. We can't put a name to the older chap, he's not on our database. By the way, Nevis, you seem to be quite a pyromaniac judging from the goings on at the Angolan Embassy earlier.'

'Don't know what you are talking about.'

'Of course you don't.'

'By the way, we have found out who the buyer of the pills destined for London is.'

'Not my problem, Nevis. Give Clancy a call.'

Click, he was gone. I'd call Clancy in the morning; it was about time I started delivering on my contract.

I spoke to Gold on the comms/. 'Talbot just met with an old client of mine. Nasty piece of work. He's left the hotel, but Talbot is still in the bar with another chap who Woodward recognises as an MI6 employee and says must be the leak.'

'Do we take them both out?' She sounded happy at the thought. It's funny how you become slanted in your thinking when you have spent a lot of your life in the killing business. It's a job, I suppose, like working in an abattoir. I couldn't do that; I couldn't kill an animal, but I can kill a human without a second thought. Yes, I know what you are thinking, dear reader, I need help – psychiatric help. Maybe, but it's war, them or us; just like the fighter pilots in WW2 trying to outdo each other with the number of 'kills' painted on their spitfire's fuselage. Those pilots didn't think about the family of the German pilot they had shot down, his kids, his parents – they couldn't afford sentiment. In certain occupations you just park sentiment and sorrow in a little room in your brain, lock the door and throw away the key. So, Gold asking if we *take them both* out seemed a normal question to ask within the framework of our business.

'No, Woodward wants to run the *leak* at Legoland and feed him false info for Erdinger. But Talbot's still dispensable. If he came to any harm FLEC would be suspected after the Embassy fire. I'll keep eyes on Talbot and Parker in the bar, and maybe a chance will come my way.'

'Talbot's not in the bar, he's in his room – he just came up in the lift.'

He must have left the bar behind me when I followed Hanson out to the foyer. 'Is he alone?'

'Yes.'

So where was Parker? I retraced my steps to the bar. It was still very busy. As I entered a scream sliced the air, and the drone of a hundred conversations fell silent. Another scream. I pushed forward through what was a mass exodus from the bar. The attentive waitress who offered to take my coat was stood beside Talbot's table, her hands clamped either side of her face and her mouth open but silent now. Justin Parker wouldn't be able to provide Woodward with a conduit for false information – Justin Parker was slumped sideways in his chair as the blood seeping from a knife wound to his heart fed a growing red patch on his shirt front. Justin Parker was dead.

No point in hanging around. The lifts were crammed full of guests getting away from the scene and seeking the safety of their rooms. I took the stairs to the seventh floor. I could boast and say I took the stairs two at a time to the seventh floor, but dear reader, fifteen years ago yes, but now maybe I could if I stopped to get my breath back every second flight. Don't get me wrong, I'm still very fit, a handful for any attacker; but that's my army training, you never forget the moves that bring your assailant down. I may lose in an arm wrestle, but in a winner takes all I'm the one who comes out alive.

On the seventh floor Gold was waiting for me by the lift – oh she of little faith! The corridor was busy with the guests hurrying to their rooms. I told her Parker was dead and Talbot must have been the killer. 'Parker probably put the pressure on him to come up with a refund to Hanson or more pills after Hanson's visit. Maybe he threatened to tell the PM what Talbot was up to if he didn't sort it. Talbot could see the whole Pyramid collapsing and panicked. I think it's time to pay Talbot an unannounced visit.'

'Never a better time than when there's a panic on,' she said with a smile. 'Ready?'

'CCTV?' I asked.

'Sorted – end of the corridor, top right corner of the ceiling.'

I turned and took a look. The CCTV lens had been sprayed white. How could I doubt her professionalism?

'Let's go.'

We walked down the corridor to room 125. Gold knocked whilst I stayed out of the peephole view.

Talbot opened the door, a look of panic on his face when he recognised Gold. 'You're not due tonight? I haven't booked you for tonight!'

'My mistake,' Gold walked forward into Talbot, flicking a foot behind his ankle and pushing him over backwards as I quickly followed her into the room, shutting the door behind me.

Talbot was kneeling and scrambling to get up. That wasn't going to happen. I put my right foot in his back and pushed him forward flat onto the floor face down as I pulled my PKK from my shoulder holster and shot him through the back of his head.

Gold checked through Talbot's briefcase; it didn't have any Pyramid paperwork. There was a tourist guide to Angola on the bedside table. I showed it to Gold.

'Optimist,' she said.

The switch blade knife he killed Parker with was in the bathroom sink. He must have been washing it when Gold knocked. It was clean, but no doubt police forensics would find some of Parker's blood on it; even the smallest molecule would identify him as the killer.

'Anything?' I asked Gold, who was checking under the mattress.

'Nothing. You want to have a go at Erdinger now?'

She was serious; so was I. 'No, we have a good scenario here. Parker killed by Talbot in the bar, and Talbot shot by Hanson. The CCTV in the bar will show them together, and with Hanson's record he'll be picked up straight away. Come on, we'd better get clear before the police arrive and shut the place down.'

The corridor was busy as we left room 125. I took the stairs and Gold took the lift.

CHAPTER 21

Gold waited patiently for the lift. The indicator showed it was stopping at every floor on its downward journey. People were leaving the hotel in droves. Funny how a great proportion of guests had no intention of being around when the police started interviewing – no doubt quite a few Mr and Mrs Smiths in the exodus. She smiled to herself. At last the lift arrived, and when the doors opened it looked full, but those already inside shuffled backwards as she and the others waiting on the seventh floor squeezed in amongst them and their luggage. Erdinger was at the back between two of his goons. One of them seemed to be paying too much attention to her. She smiled and turned her back towards them, wishing she had put her PKK in her jacket pocket and not the Burberry. Her comms earpiece was hidden out of sight under her hair and the mic clipped onto her lapel. You would have to look closely to see it. If Erdinger was leaving the hotel, which he probably was, he was travelling light. But then he hadn't arrived with any luggage from his hasty retreat from the Embassy, so he should be. It took an age for the lift to reach the ground floor, stopping at all six floors on the way. She spilled out with the other guests and walked away from the front doors as just about everybody else, including Erdinger's trio, headed towards them. She stood by the reception desk, mingling with the guests checking out as she watched Erdinger's trio in the big wall mirrors. No telltale sign of either of the goons taking an interest in her. They were intent on forcing a way through the throng for their boss.

'Erdinger's on the move, he's leaving,' she alerted Nevis. Last thing they wanted was Nevis to be recognised by one of the goons. 'Where are you?'

'I'm out. See you at the car.'

'Okay.' Gold circled the foyer and left inside a crowd hustling to grab a taxi. Funny how the London taxi drivers grapevine gets wind of things happening where taxis are wanted even before the emergency services. The queue of *For Hire* roof lights already stretched back out of the hotel access road and along the Albert Embankment.

Gold flicked on the tracker app. It was flashing but static. Erdinger's car was stationary on the Albert Embankment. The crush of taxis had prevented the driver getting right up to the hotel doors. That was good; it gave her and Nevis time to get to the Kia.

CHAPTER 22

'Where the hell is he going?' I asked Gold.

We had followed Erdinger through the West End, through the City and onto the Poplar Road heading east.

'God knows,' was her helpful reply. 'Essex?'

'Why? It doesn't make sense, unless he's heading for the coast?'

'Pick up a boat and cross the Channel?'

'Could be. Hold on.' The tracker turned right off the A13 into Prince Regent Lane. 'Take the next right.' That could only mean one destination that Erdinger was heading for. 'London City Airport! He's going to catch a plane, got to be – nothing else this way.' She accelerated and turned down Prince Regent Lane. The tracker showed Erdinger's car swing left at the crossroads, and then right down Connaught Bridge. That road doesn't go anywhere else, just to the airport. I watched the red dot on the tracker. 'He's going round the back.' At the far side of the airport are the hangars; not the major airline hangars, most belong to flying clubs and courier services, plus the heliport is there too.

Gold drove around the perimeter road a good couple of hundred metres behind Erdinger. We stopped as he turned into the rear security gate and a guard came out of the gatehouse and had words before he waved to his partner inside, and the barrier raised for Erdinger's car to go through.

'You park up somewhere. I'll sneak in and find out what he's up to. If he's taking a flight out we need to know where he's going.'

'Okay, take care. Keep in contact.'

I reached into the Burberry and took out a balaclava and pulled it on before slipping out of the car. I removed my jacket and put it on the front seat with Woodward's phone. I was now all in black – even my shoulder holster was black leather; I felt good, ready for work.

I made my way towards the gate, keeping close to the steel wall. The Security people were inside their pod watching television. They wouldn't have much to do this time of night, and the speed with which Erdinger's car was let through without any paperwork being checked meant it was expected. It was simple to duck down below the gatehouse windows and enter the airport proper.

The tall hangars loomed up in front of me, eight in a row. I hurried along the alleyway between two of them towards the runway and peeped round to the front. The only activity was on the helipad; a Sikorsky S-76 waited expectantly with its lights on and two pilots in position behind the controls. The side door was open, with a short stepladder positioned beneath it. Erdinger wasn't going to Angola in it, as the maximum journey of the S-76 is four hundred and fifty miles, so where was he off to? I needed to find out.

I told Gold what I'd seen and gave her the helicopter's registration number painted on its tail. A shaft of light was coming from one of the hangars that had the roller door up far enough to walk in. I moved closer and voices came from inside, but I couldn't make out what they were saying. I moved closer, hugging the wall, and stole a look inside. A group of men including Erdinger were talking in a far corner. I struggled to hear what they were saying.

I didn't struggle to hear what the voice behind was saying.

'Raise your hands slowly and put them on your head – and don't make any silly moves or you will be killed. There are two of us.'

The Eastern European accent matched the one I'd heard at the Guildhall caper. I felt the tip of a pistol press against my neck through the balaclava and a hand reach around my body and slip my PKK from my shoulder holster. If I was going to fight it had to be now, but if there were two of them it would just be futile. Maybe he was lying and was alone, but you don't take that chance.

The voice shouted something to the group of men in the far corner in a foreign language. It sounded German, but I wasn't sure. I still had the comms in place with the mic on, so hoped Gold was aware of what was happening.

The group walked across the empty hangar to join us. Erdinger said something, definitely in German. One of his men jerked the balaclava off my head, followed by my earpiece and the mic. They were dropped on the concrete floor and crushed under foot.

Erdinger looked at me for several seconds as if trying to place my face.

'So you must be Mr Portman. Not your real name, of course. A mercenary, a hired gun.' He looked me in the eye, and his eyes showed a contemptuous hatred. 'You killed my son, Mr Portman, so I am going to kill you. I would like to take my time over killing you, but your paymasters at FLEC have caused me some inconvenience that I need to put right. They won't win, of course, but you won't be around to see them fail. Goodbye, Mr Portman.'

Well, at least the graffiti on the Embassy wall had worked. Perhaps I could give Banksy a run for his money if I got out of here alive? Erdinger nodded to the men behind me. I waited for the bullet I knew I wouldn't feel. Oh well, let's hope Gold gets clear and avenges my death. I didn't feel the bullet; I felt a needle penetrate my neck instead.

CHAPTER 23

Gold parked the car against the Thames Embankment wall. The river flowed past shimmering in the moonlight, cold and uninviting. She had heard Erdinger on the comms before the signal went dead. Nothing had been said about her, so with luck Erdinger's people thought Nevis was working alone. She had to get inside the airport and see what was happening. Surprise would be on her side.

She left the car, and like Nevis removed her jacket and checked her shoulder holster. She took flash-bang sticks from the Burberry; always good for creating a distraction when you need one.

The unmistakable noise of a helicopter rotor came from the airport direction, and it was getting louder. She grabbed the binoculars and focused on it as the S-76 came into view, rising above the hangars, and swept round towards her position. She looked at the registration; it was Erdinger's. Was Nevis on board, or was his body lying somewhere on the tarmac? She watched as the copter headed her way and veered left over the river and then hovered. Had she been seen? She ducked away from the car and watched from the shadow of a large tree.

The side door of the helicopter opened, sending out a shaft of light. Gold expected a few shots from an AK-47 maybe to come her way. Nothing, then activity at the door as a bundle was pushed out, and she followed it as it fell. There was no mistaking what it was by the arms and legs flailing loosely in the air before it splashed into the Thames. The door on the copter shut and it veered right across the Thames, gained height and flew away into the distance.

Gold was already over the concrete flood wall in the murky Thames and swimming towards where the splash had been.

CHAPTER 24

I blinked a few times to clear the mist from my eyes. I was seeing a light, the sort of light you see at the dentist, a light that doesn't hurt your eyes. What was I doing at a dentist's? I didn't understand. I was lying down. The fog in my brain cleared as the light moved away, and a face appeared and lingered above me. A female face wearing a COVID mask. The face spoke from behind the mask.

'He's back with us now.'

The face withdrew from sight and another took its place.

'Wakey wakey, Ben,' Gold said with a smile.

My mind clicked into gear as hands and arms lifted me into a sitting position, and I saw I was in a cotton gown and on a slim mattress on a large operating table in the middle of what looked like a hospital operating theatre. The pages of memory clicked through in my mind up to the point of being in the London City Airport hangar, and then nothing.

'How are you feeling?' asked the woman in the mask. She was older than Gold, late middle-age with deep blue eyes that held mine as I looked at her. She was in a green hospital nurse trouser suit. Was I in hospital? Why was I in hospital? I didn't feel any pain.

'I feel okay. Where am I?'

'You are at the vet's.' Gold's smile was now much wider and almost breaking into a laugh.

My mind scrambled – *the vet's*? What did she mean *the vets*? Was I in a military veterans' hospital?

'How much do you remember?' she asked.

'The hangar,' I said. 'Seeing Erdinger and his goons in the hangar.'

'You don't remember being in the helicopter?'

'No, I remember seeing it but nothing else.'

'Okay, relax and listen.'

The woman in the mask put pillows under my head and I lay back as Gold took me through the events. She had overheard the conversation in the hangar through my comms, and she had heard Erdinger tell his people to put me in the copter. She didn't know I was unconscious by then and had watched it take off, realising what had happened to me when I was thrown out over the Thames. Couldn't be anybody else, could it? She had dived in, pulled me out and pumped the

Thames from my stomach. I was alive, but not responding because of the drug in my body.

'Ketamine,' said the mask. 'Injected it knocks you out immediately. I've given you a dose of benzodiazepines which negates its effect. You may get dizzy until it moves through the system.'

'I don't want to appear rude, 'I said. 'But who are you?'

Gold explained. 'She is Rachel Abelman – Doctor Rachel Abelman. Ex-Mossad, took a sniper's bullet out of my back in Afghanistan. Now has a practice here in London.'

Knowing Gold's military past, that made sense. 'And which hospital are we in?'

'We are not in a hospital, I told you – you're at the vet's.'

I was getting the picture. 'As in dogs and cats?'

'Yes – imagine the questions and paperwork involved if I'd taken you to a hospital? What name to use for a start – where's your NHS record? Have you even got one? Probably still be waiting to be seen now, or sitting in an ambulance parked outside. Rachel looks after me and several other ex-Mossad in the UK who wish to remain under the radar.'

I could understand that. Dick Clancy had told me about two vets who regularly stitch up human wounds with no questions asked; in the early days of the London gang wars fighting for turf where they could deal the E pills, dealers got knifed and shot. A very profitable time for those two vets.

The mask spoke. 'Welcome to the Highgate Veterinary Practice, Ben.'

'Thank you.' I made a note to check myself over when I could. Didn't want to find I'd been neutered.

'Right.' Gold was getting impatient. 'We have work to do. I checked the copter's flight plan, it was heading for Manchester.'

'Whoa!' The mask held up a hand. 'Ben needs a day to fully recover, I'd put everything on hold until tomorrow if I were you.'

I looked around the room; no clock. 'What is the time?'

Gold checked her watch. 'Seven a.m.'

The mask was right. I felt that I needed a few hours to get myself together, check in with Woodward, and just get back on track.

'Has Woodward phoned?'

Gold nodded. 'Several times, but I haven't answered. It's in the car.'

'My clothes?'

‘Jacket’s in the car, and your jumper and trousers should be dry enough to wear.’ She pointed to them, draped over a radiator with my socks and underwear. My shoes stood on the floor beside them. ‘Get dressed, and I’ll be in reception. Out of the door, turn right, and it’s at the end of the corridor.’

Highgate Veterinary Practice was a big operation; Rachel Abelman had done well for herself. The corridor was fifty metres and the doors off it were marked Operating Theatre, three of, Scanner, two of, Recovery Ward, four of, Pharmacy, one of, Staff Only, two of. And there were two other corridors leading off the large, plush reception area where the mask and Gold were waiting for me.

We said our goodbyes and thank yous.

‘What about the bill?’ I asked Gold as we walked to her Kia in the car park. I was apprehensive of the answer, as I know from experience what vet’s bills are like. Think of a number, double it, and then add two zeros.

‘All sorted.’

I thought thanks were in order. ‘You saved my life.’

‘I did. Just part of the job, Ben.’ She smiled. ‘You’d do the same for me.’

I let that hang in the air for a few seconds before replying. ‘I can’t swim.’

CHAPTER 25

Gold dropped me off at Annie Greggs's CRV. No parking ticket? I had expected one at least. The genuine owner of the registration plate would have had a shock if one had been issued. I drove back to my apartment, parking two blocks away, took a long hot shower and made myself a thick bacon sandwich. God, that tasted good! Woodward's phone was buzzing every ten minutes; he must have it on repeat mode. He wasn't going to interrupt my bacon sandwich. Feeling peckish, dear reader? I bet you are – I don't know anybody who can resist the thought of a bacon sandwich. Setting religious choices aside that is.

I finished with a Colombian bean coffee from the percolator and waited for Woodward's next try. I know, I usually push the delight of a French bean coffee, but Mehmet pushed a Colombian at me and I have to say he certainly knows my tastes. Stronger than the French bean, but not strong enough to be edging towards bitter. Try it.

Woodward's phone buzzed. I answered, 'Early Retirement Planning, how can we help?'

He ignored it as usual. 'The reason you have a direct line phone from me, Nevis, is so that I can contact you and you me, for immediate response.

'I was working.' I didn't feel like taking him through the London City Airport episode.

'Yes, so I gather from the carnage in your wake. Anymore arson episodes or bodies likely to come to light that I don't know about?'

'Which do you know about?'

'The Angolan Embassy fire and the murder of a member of my staff in the Park Plaza.'

'You missed out Talbot.'

'What about Talbot?'

'He's dead. I shot him in his hotel room at the Plaza.'

There was a short silence. 'Clancy's people checked his hotel room after Parker's killing. It was empty.'

There was only one answer. 'It's been cleaned then. I left him there with the knife he stabbed Parker with lying in the bathroom sink. Erdinger's sent the cleaners in. Why would he do that?'

'Because things are moving fast, Nevis, very fast. Do you know where Erdinger is now?'

'Manchester. I'll be going up there later.' I had arranged to meet Gold in the afternoon.

'Correct, Erdinger is in Manchester – he's there to chair a hastily arranged meeting of the UK Pyramid group in the Midland Hotel. He's not stupid. Nevis – he's lost a number of his couriers in the Luanda explosion, plus several of his men despatched by you in London, and now, if, as you say, Talbot is dead, he has lost his top man in the UK, his PM in waiting.'

'Talbot is definitely dead.'

'Then he's panicking. I would guess he's bringing in the far right much quicker than he'd like. He's going to stir up the UK political pot and create unrest. Insurgents feed on unrest.'

'Pull him in, get Clancy to arrest him on terrorism charges.'

'No, that would just get him the opportunity to feed the flames of his revolution through the courts. Probably get bail anyway. No, I suggest you fulfil your contract, Nevis, with speed.'

'Okay.'

'The Foreign Office has instructed our ambassadors in the countries where Erdinger has built influence to have a quiet word with those currently in power and warn them of the imminent threat of the Pyramid groups operating in their countries. I am pretty sure there will be quite a few Pyramid members quietly disappearing, and others taken into custody to face charges of insurrection.'

'You've got all your ducks in row now, haven't you.'

'I hope so, Nevis. Good luck.'

Click, and he was gone.

I rang Gold and told her to book a room for herself in Manchester, but not at the Midland Hotel. I rang the Midland and booked my room. Gold was going to drive up but I didn't trust Annie Greggs's rental car to make it up the motorway, so I booked a train ticket from Euston online. I ordered an Uber to meet me outside a block two streets down and we called at Gilbert Charles's on the way with a shopping list Gold had given me. More flash-bangs, smoke canisters, Semtex sticks and fuses. She wasn't leaving anything to chance, was she?

Gilbert smiled a knowing smile as he handed me the McDonald's bag in exchange for a wad of twenty pound notes. 'Ten o'clock news should be worth watching tonight then?'

'I couldn't possible comment, Gilbert.'

He laughed. 'You take care, Ben.'

CHAPTER 26

I booked into the Midland late in the afternoon as Mr Lakenheath; I thought Portman had run its course, and Erdinger's people would be surprised and alerted if they saw it in the register. As far as they were concerned, I was at the bottom of the Thames.

There weren't any advertising boards about a Pyramid meeting, but as Woodward had said, it was a hastily convened one, so not pre-booked.

I checked in with Gold. She was in the Town House, her car in the multi-storey. I told her to come over later in the evening and take a stroll around the bars in the Midland to see if she recognised anybody. I didn't want to show myself as too many of Erdinger's goons might know my face by now. No doubt my mugshot had been circulated after Talbot's demise.

The thing with Gold is that she's too bloody good at her job. She knocked at my room at 8.30 that evening with a smile on her face.

'They are all here.'

'Who's 'all'?'

She sat beside me on the bed and took a small collection of cards the size of playing cards from the Burberry. Each one had a mugshot pasted to it and a description along the bottom.

'These are all booked in.' She passed them to me. I recognised some of the faces and all the descriptions.

'Where did you get these?'

'The Met's proscribed groups file.'

I gave her a look that said, *'Don't say another word, I don't want to know how you hacked into that.'*

It seemed Erdinger was in the company of representatives from National Action, Britain First, British Democrats, Patriotic Alternative, Homeland, The English Defence League, and The British Freedom Party.

'We can't kill all that lot.' I was racking my brain for an answer. Erdinger had to be taken out, that was the brief, but not all this lot.

'Why not? They are in all proscribed groups, all banned from meeting, and here they are holding a conference! By the way, their meeting with Erdinger is tomorrow at 11 a.m. in committee room four, ground floor.'

I was impressed. 'How do you know that?'

'Two of them talking at the bar.'

Woodward's mobile buzzed.

I answered it. 'Meals on Wheels, was there a problem with your soup?'

He ignored it. 'Sky nine o'clock news, and a reminder that your target is still in play.' Click, and he was gone.

'Your target is still in play.' What was that about? Erdinger was my target, I knew that.

I told Gold what he had said and she shrugged. She didn't know what he meant either. I pressed the buttons on the TV remote and the screen on the wall lit up. I scrolled to Sky News. We had three minutes until nine o'clock. The usual adverts were running so I boiled the kettle and hoisted hotel tea bags into two cups. The water turned a sort of pale beige, so I added two more bags. No difference.

Gold stepped over and took a look.

'I'll give that a miss.'

I agreed and emptied the cups down the sink in the bathroom. The Sky News music was playing as I came back and watched.

The media were outside the Angolan Embassy. Clancy's Organised Crime officers were bringing out a handcuffed ambassador and staff and loading them into police vans.

The journalist explained to camera whilst the action went on behind him. 'The Organised Crime Squad this evening raided the Angolan

Embassy here in London to break an international drug smuggling ring involving the Ambassador and the international movement of stolen Angolan diamonds used to purchase fentanyl and cocaine from cartels in South America. We understand raids are taking place in several other countries in Europe and Africa where this international gang has established a foothold using a fake international company known as Pyramid. We have been told enquiries are ongoing and more arrests are imminent.'

So, nothing about the political aspirations of Pyramid? I could see what Woodward was doing. If he kept the operation within the organised crime sphere as far as the media was concerned, then he and the anti-terrorism police in the other countries involved could quietly mop up the Pyramid's political wings as organised crime and keep politics out of it. I also understood his line about *'your target is still in play'* now. Erdinger would have seen or been told what was happening in London. He and his little band of insurgents would be packing and leaving the hotel, if they hadn't already done so, and Erdinger would be going underground; Woodward wanted a quick resolution before he did. I ran that thought past Gold; she agreed, and we took our PKKs from the Burberry, checked the magazines and left the room. She took the lift and I took the stairs. If Erdinger was going to do a runner we needed to be around to follow him. '*Your target is still in play*,' ran through my mind as I made my way down the staircase. Woodward wanted Erdinger rubbed out ASAP.

The Hotel foyer was a surprise. Yes, Erdinger's little band of nasties had indeed packed and fled, or tried to. Trouble was, they only fled into the arms of overwhelming numbers of MOD Police in fully armed combat dress, who had them held in line, handcuffed and being joined by others as they left the foyer lifts to be arrested. Woodward had designated this part of his operation to the MOD; he had Clancy and his Organised Crime unit handling the Embassy, and now the MOD handling this end. Crafty bugger, eh? Don't show your hand unless you have to was obviously his playbook in this operation. I waited outside the street doors until Gold joined me.

'I've been made.' She looked worried.

I assumed she didn't mean she'd been promoted to be a Mafia Don.

'Who by?'

'One of Erdinger's men. He gave me a good stare back at the Plaza in London, and I thought he might have recognised me then, but he was in the lift just now. It was packed, but he definitely made me – I could almost hear the sirens going off in his brain.'

'Where is he?' My immediate thought was to somehow eliminate this goon so he couldn't alert Erdinger.

'Stayed in the lift when he saw what was happening in the foyer, went back up.'

'Well, if he did recognise you, Erdinger now knows too, and he'll put two and two together and realise somebody is onto him.'

'He thinks you're at the bottom of the Thames.'

'Yes, but he's going to be ultra careful now, isn't he? Talbot dead, the Angolan Ambassador arrested, that lot in the foyer rounded up, and maybe one of his men recognising you.'

'He'll go down a bolt hole. People like him always have an exit worked out.'

'Woodward will have his picture with the Border Force, so he won't be able to legally leave the country – and he'll know that. He's not stupid enough to turn up at Customs departures.'

'So, where's he going to go? He can't use the Embassy anymore.'

There was only one place, it hit me like a lightning bolt. 'Hanson's!'

'Hanson's?'

'Of course, Jimmy Hanson is the man who buys his drugs, and they both need each other. Hanson's business is cut-throat, if he hasn't any drugs for his dealers he's out of the game and somebody else will muscle in – and that 'somebody else' will have their own supplier and won't need Erdinger, which means he'll have no income. Got to be Hanson, they need each other to survive.' I could see by Gold's face she wasn't a hundred percent sold on my reading of the situation. 'You don't agree?'

'Long shot.'

'So was Foinavon at a hundred to one for the National, but he won.'

'What?'

'Never mind. Come on, back to London and I'll make a few enquiries.'

'We could take out Erdinger here before he leaves. You know what Woodward said.'

'Yes, but he'll be gone by now, and he only has one safe exit route left, Jimmy Hanson. Where's your car?'

'At the Town House.'

'Come on. We need to find Hanson before he spirits Erdinger away.'

'Do you know where he is?'

‘No, but I know a man who will.’

CHAPTER 27

Dawn was breaking when we got back to London. Gold dropped me off at Victoria and I took a black cab to two streets away from my apartment building and checked Annie's car was still there; it was, of course. I walked the rest of the way; nobody followed me.

'A good night was it, Mr Halford?' The front desk security guards gave me knowing smiles that related to their impression I was returning from some sort of depraved 'all-nighter'.

I ignored it. 'Anybody looking for me?'

'No.'

'Good.'

I took a shower, set the alarm for 11.45 a.m. and slept like a log. Even in the Middle Eastern conflicts, with ordnance flying all around, I could curl up in a fox hole and be in the land of nod in minutes.

It seemed like only minutes until the buzzing of the alarm clock pulled me from slumberland. I took a wash, two slices of Marmite on toast and a coffee before checking the midday television news. It was still leading with the Angolan Embassy affair, with a follow-up piece about the Manchester arrests. They had it as a terrorism clamp down on the activities of proscribed groups in the UK who had been meeting at the Midland. The law doesn't allow members of such groups to hold meetings, so I assume that's what they'll be charged with. Depending on the mood of the judge, they'll either get a hefty fine or go down for a couple of years and be out after one. Looks good for public consumption, but the public won't know the real reason behind the Manchester meeting. Smoke and mirrors.

I turned the television off and gave Annie Greggs a call.

She managed to say 'Hello lover boy...' in a poor Marilyn Monroe to JFK impersonation before the smoker's cough that rattling up from her tar-covered lungs took over. She croaked and spluttered away from the phone for a while before coming back. 'Fucking cheap foreign fags from the fucking street market, he said they was English. I'll kill the cunt.' Then back to the Marilyn Monroe impersonation that sounded more like Kathy Burke, unless Monroe was actually a cockney? 'I knew you couldn't resist me, Ben. But it will have to be a long-term commitment – I'm not a one night stand girl.'

I laughed. 'You are a cheeky bugger, Annie. I actually want to have a word with Jimmy if he's back in the fold?'

'Of course he's back – when his *true-love* found out he's a skint old lag with new knees and fifteen years older than he told her, he was out the door. Hang on.'

I could hear her telling Jimmy I was on the phone for him.

'Allo?'

'Jimmy, it's Ben. I want a bit of information.'

'Hello, Ben. Go on.'

'What's Jimmy Hanson up to these days, and where's he working from?'

'You got a death wish, Ben? You don't muck about with that bloke.'

'I know, I did some work for him years ago. Don't worry, Jimmy, all I want to know is where I can find him if I need to.'

'Don't mention my name.'

'Of course not.'

'Last I heard he was using a warehouse in Milkwood Road, Herne Hill, importing furniture – at least, that's the cover, I don't think he actually imports anything, but it's handy for distributing what you and I know he's into, right?'

'Right.'

'He's top man now, Ben, and he didn't get there by being nice to the other dealers. He has every night club tied up with his bouncers on the doors, so only his dealers get in.'

I knew Jimmy Blunt from way back when he was one of those bouncers. 'Who's he working with?'

Jimmy laughed. 'Nobody. He tied up with Louis Constantine, remember him?'

'Yes.' I do remember Louis; he had a few Greek restaurants in the West End. 'I didn't know he was into drug dealing?'

'He wasn't. Hanson tied up with him to launder money through the restaurants, but it seems Louis skimmed a bit too much off the top and got caught. All of a sudden the restaurants were up for sale, Louis had disappeared, and his family had gone home to Greece. Rumour was that he went to sea in a chicken wire suit.'

You, dear reader, won't know what a chicken wire suit is. In the time Jimmy is talking about London was still in the era of gang warfare, and battles over drug turfs were common. Quite a few gangsters were *disappeared*, and one way of getting rid of the bodies was to strip them, weigh them down with lead bricks, wrap them in chicken wire and drop them overboard in the middle of the English Channel. If the sea creatures didn't devour them through the wire, the bodies would decompose quite quickly in salt water.

'Thanks, Jimmy – useful information. Tell Annie I'll return her car soon.'

'Okay, Ben – take care, mate. You're in dangerous territory with Hanson.'

I clicked off. Hanson had to be helping Erdinger, it made perfect sense.

CHAPTER 28

I shifted my backside. We had been sat in Gold's Kia at the end of the interior delivery road of Milkwood Road Industrial Estate in Herne Hill for three hours, and I was getting stiff. I checked my watch: 4.30 p.m. Hanson's unit had been quiet. A couple of shifty looking characters with hoodies had been in and out, most likely street drug dealers paying in or collecting more pills. No sign of Hanson or Erdinger, or Erdinger's car either. The tracker's battery had run out so it could be anywhere. Gold had checked the underground garage near the Embassy to fit a new one, but the car wasn't there. I was getting a little worried that I'd made the wrong call. Perhaps Hanson hadn't given Erdinger a temporary home? In that case, Erdinger could be anywhere. My thought that Hanson would help Erdinger had made perfect sense standing outside the Midland Hotel in Manchester, but wasn't making perfect sense now sitting in a South London industrial estate fighting cramp. My mobile buzzed; it was Clancy. I put it on speaker.

'How long are you going to sit there?'

'Sit where?'

'In an industrial estate watching Hanson's unit – he's not there, nor is Erdinger. Hanson's on his way back from Belgium, probably with a case full of fentanyl pills to replace the ones that Woodward's people seized in Luanda. I don't know where Erdinger is, but he's not with Hanson.'

I took a quick look around. I couldn't see anybody else. A couple of trucks and cars, but all looked empty. 'Where are you?'

'Sitting in my office at West End Central.'

That could only mean one thing. 'So you got a surveillance team on Hanson's unit then?'

'Of course – lots of CCTV cameras in that estate, Ben, but which are ours, eh?' He laughed. 'Hanson is *numero uno* in the London drugs trade. We've been watching him for three months and compiling a list of all his contacts and every visitor to the premises. So don't you go and muck it up in your quest for Erdinger. Hanson is not designated as possible collateral damage.'

'Save the cost of a trial.'

'And how would I explain to the Home Secretary? *'Yes, ma'am, we had him under surveillance for three months, and then somebody else stepped in and killed him'*. Wouldn't look like our surveillance was much good, would it, Ben? Erdinger is yours and Woodward's, Hanson is ours. If we get a sighting of Erdinger I'll let you know. Have you checked out Hanson's home?'

No I hadn't. Jimmy Blunt hadn't mentioned anything about Hanson's home. 'No, where is that?'

'West Mersea'

'Never heard of it – Liverpool way?'

'No, lots of people make that assumption. It's on Mersea Island, off the Essex coast near Colchester – not the River Mersey in Liverpool. The island is said to be the place where the Romans first landed – famous for its oysters. Hanson has got a big place in West Mersea, that's the inhabited part – small population, mainly locals and a few incoming rich. I'll look up his address and text it to you. East Mersea is the other half of the island – wildlife conservancy, area of outstanding natural beauty. You get to it over a causeway you can drive over at low tide, but beware, the tide cuts it off twice a day. Have a nice time, Ben – don't forget your bucket and spade.' Click, and he was gone.

Gold had Googled Mersea Island on her phone. 'A12 to Colchester and turn right. We have two hours before the tide comes in, yes?' She raised her eyebrows questioningly.

I nodded. 'Yes.'

CHAPTER 29

The slowest part of the trip was getting through London's rush hour traffic. Once we were onto the A12 it quickened up, and each time we passed a junction and some of the commuters turned off, the snake of cars thinned out more and Gold was able to speed up. We hit Colchester at a quarter to six; Mersea Island was well signposted with the roads skirting the City, and by ten past we approached the causeway Clancy had mentioned. It was a five hundred metre single lane concrete road between the mainland and the island. The homeward bound commuters from Colchester presented a long line of cars that claimed it one way onto the island. Three cars waiting at the other end to come off would have a long wait.

I looked at the postcode Clancy had texted and put it into the Kia's sat nav. The screen showed a road at the far edge of the island bordering the River Blackwater estuary. The sat nav took us into the west area, past a small shopping area in narrow roads and then down a short twisting hill to the beach road. 'You have reached your destination' said the lady in the sat nav. The road was dark, with the only light coming from street lamps erected on the drives by the owners of the large Victorian properties spread out along it; some were gated. I checked Clancy's text on my phone.

'We are looking for a place called 'Molly's.'

Gold gave a laugh. 'Cheeky, eh?'

'Very.'

For those dear readers who aren't aware of the connection, Molly isn't the name of Hanson's wife; as far as I know he's not married. No, 'Molly', as well as being a female's name, is also the street name for the drug ecstasy, the drug that made Hanson his first fortune in the 80's. By naming his house 'Molly', he is basically holding up two fingers to Clancy and his Organised Crime Unit, much like John Palmer did in the early 80's with his two dogs, Brinks and Mat.

'Got to be that one.' Gold nodded towards a large bay windowed house set well back behind a shrubbery. The drive was closed to the road by an ornate, fifteen foot-high steel gate, and high railings separated the property from the road. Sat on the drive in full view was a burgundy Range Rover.

'They must have found the tracker,' I reasoned.

'Could have malfunctioned.'

'Well, at least we know where Erdinger is now.'

We drove on past three more large houses to the end of the road, which petered out into a dirt turning circle and parking area with a sign that read 'Beach' pointing down a sloping footpath between some scrub. The sound of the waves playing with the beach pebbles meant we were close to the shore.

Gold heaved the Burberry over from the back seat. 'The full kit?' she asked.

'I think so.' Boy Scouts aren't the only ones who believe in being prepared.

We checked our PKKs, screwed on silencers, took a second magazine of .45 bullets, two flash bangs each, one six-inch stick of Semtex with a fuse, a pair of black gloves, black balaclava, night vision goggles, and checked our comms were working okay. I slung my light colour jacket onto the back seat and we left the car, silently closing the doors.

We took the footpath down to the beach and kept high on it, moving along the ground above the pebbles. If you have ever tried to run on beach pebbles you'll know why; plus they are noisy to walk on. None of the houses were very secure at the back. A six foot-high sea wall with a thick steel door protected each of them from a rogue high tide; over that wall and you were into their back gardens. Some nice motorboats were anchored in the water just off the shore line; there was obviously some money on this island. All the houses had a large rear balcony extending from the upper floor that would give magnificent sea views. But this was September, and although lights shone from inside some of the houses, I couldn't see anybody outside enjoying the balcony view. A lone dog barked a few times as we passed the second house. At Hanson's we stopped and sat down in the shade of the sea wall.

'I'll go in, you cover me,' I said. 'If Erdinger's inside he is bound to have a couple of his goons for company.'

'Okay, I'll be around.'

I knew she would be. In fact, I had relied on Gold *being around* a few times in the past, and she always had been.

The steel door from the beach to the rear garden was padlocked, so I scaled the wall and dropped into a shrubbery. I waited immobile for a minute, taking in the layout. The shrubs gave way to a lawn that led to the back of the house that was covered on the ground floor by a long conservatory lit with hanging fluorescent lights. Perhaps Hanson was a keen gardener? The conservatoire looked to have plenty of greenery inside, most likely marijuana. Either side of the house a path ran through to the front; he paths were made of beach pebbles, so you couldn't use them without making the clacking noise of pebble against pebble as you did. So the conservatory was my only way in.

I skirted the garden and approached it from the side that had a door. It wasn't locked. I quarter-opened it and listened. All was quiet. I was tempted by purple grapes hanging in bunches from a vine that wound its way across the roof on poles. I was right about the marijuana; they were in closely packed pots with hanging heaters keeping the conservatory at the required temperature. A double door led from the conservatory into the house, it was shut. I kept to the house wall of the conservatory, moving carefully between the plants, out of the light as much as possible.

At the door I peeped through into the house. The room was a large spacious lounge; the light was on but nobody was inside. I silently and slowly opened one of the doors and moved inside. A button leather three piece suite plus two extra chairs was all the furniture. In the middle an expensive misted glass coffee table sat on the wall-to-wall deep red carpet. Handy for disguising blood stains if Hanson had to discipline somebody - or worse. I moved around the side of the room to a closed door which I reckoned would lead out to a hallway. It did; to the left were two more rooms off the hallway with doors closed, and then at the end the front door to the house. To the right, along the corridor, an open door off that led into a kitchen where the light was on, and a flight of dark stairs going up to what must be the bedrooms, including the back one with the large balcony.

A noise from the kitchen caused me to close the lounge door so I had just a slit to look through. More noise; the recognisable sound of china cups clinking together. A goon carrying a tray with three cups came to the kitchen door from inside; he paused, flicked off the light and took the stairs. So there were three of them. Well, maybe four if one of the party upstairs didn't want a drink. I've learnt to read the signs, like the number of drinks going into a room can give you an indication of how many adversaries there are – but only an indication, never take it as gospel!

The goon disappeared at the top of the stairs and I heard voices and occasional laughter. I stuck close to the wall as I moved slowly up the stairs. The room where the voices were coming from was five metres along the landing. The door was half open, spilling light out onto the dark landing. I moved in a crouch position to the door and spied through the crack between the half open door and the wall. Three men were in the room. One sat on a large double bed reading a paper; one stood by the open double glass doors to the balcony smoking, and Erdinger sat in a comfy armchair looking at a sheaf of papers in his hand, turning the pages over slowly. A chandelier hung from the centre of the ceiling and its candle-shaped bulbs threw light around the room. The tea from the kitchen was being sipped, so the conversation was on hold. I weighed up my options. I could burst in and shoot them all, relying on surprise to shift the odds in my favour. They would undoubtedly have pistols in shoulder holsters, so my shots would have to count. Whatever I did it had to be quick, before they could react. I didn't think Erdinger would have a gun, so he would be my last kill. It was a gamble though, he might be armed.

I had another trick up my sleeve: my night goggles. I moved my head and looked at the wall beside the door. Victorian houses always had the light switches on the wall beside the door on the opening side at shoulder height. This house was no exception, and the switch stood proud from the wall. I smiled to myself – thank you, Mr Hanson, for not updating the house lighting.

I stood and edged towards it under the cover of the door, took a deep breath, flipped down the night goggles and took a fast step forward into the light and the room, flicking off the switch with my left hand, swivelling round to face the room and sliding down to a crouch position against the wall. My view was now a dark green blanket, with three yellow figures and a lighter green of the double door to the balcony and the lighter night sky. I raised my PKK and, using the standard double-handed grip, took out the man on the bed who pitched forward onto the floor as the bullet crashed into his skull above the right ear and out of it from above his left ear – the exit wound would have left a gaping hole for his brains to slowly exit.

The second man couldn't decide whether to put his tea cup and saucer on the table or just drop them. He should have just dropped them and gone for his gun. My second bullet hit him in the heart and he dropped them anyway, the cup and saucer hitting the floor at the same time he did. Bullets to the body don't always kill, even when to the heart, so I pumped another one into his forehead as he hit the floor. The green figure of Erdinger hadn't moved, probably frozen in shock. I pushed my night goggles up and flicked the light switch back on. The chandelier lit up his frightened face as he saw me coming towards him. He went to get up from the chair. I shot his right knee and he howled and slumped back down, clutching it. The negotiation started.

'I've got money,' was his opening gambit.

'I'm sure you have,' I replied. 'But I don't think there's a charge to get into Hell.'

He snarled. 'You're Nevis, aren't you. Parker told me you were the one.'

'The one?'

'The one who killed my son.'

'When you see him, tell him I said hello.' I raised my gun and killed Alaric Erdinger with one bullet to the brain. Job done. I don't know why I said what I did, been watching too many Netflix gangster shows probably. *'Tell him I said hello'* – not even original, eh?

Phutt! The sound of a silenced shot from outside the balcony doors brought me back to the present situation. I swung round, kneeling down and aiming my PKK at the doors. It seemed an age, but was just a couple of seconds in real time before an upright figure fell from the side of the left door like a falling telegraph pole onto the balcony floor, his dead hand clamped onto a pistol. His eyes stared into nothing from under the hole that was a .45 calibre exit wound in his forehead.

Silence... then Gold's voice from the garden, calm and collected. 'All clear.'

Shit! There *had* been a third goon, one who obviously didn't want a cup of tea. He was on the balcony when I burst in, probably having a cigarette. I got to my feet and walked across to the balcony, stepping over his body, and looked down through the railings along the balcony front. Gold stood below in the garden, pistol in hand.

'Thanks.' I gave her a smile.

'You're welcome. Next?'

'Come up and we'll have a quick think.'

Gold joined me in the bedroom. She admired the chandelier.

'Who said crime doesn't pay.'

'The type of crime Hanson is involved in pays very well.'

'Time to go, isn't it?'

'Can't leave four bodies.'

'That's Hanson's problem, his house.'

'Clancy doesn't want him involved, they've got a big Interpol gig in play. Hanson's one of the big boys in the middle. The last thing they want is for him to cut and run.'

'You mean we are going to have to clean this up? Are we taking four bodies all the way back to London to the magicians?'

'No, I've a better idea. Help me chuck this lot over the balcony.'

She shrugged and grabbed the third goon's feet as I lifted him by the arms, and we swung him twice before aiming him over the balcony railings. As we let him go, I had one terrible thought, if the conservatory below extended beyond the width of the balcony, there was going to be an almighty crash of breaking glass. There wasn't. I looked over; the conservatory couldn't be seen, the balcony covered it and few feet more.

One by one we pitched the other three bodies over. I stood catching my breath once we finished; Gold wasn't even breathing heavily. I told myself she's younger.

A telephone rang. We looked around. It was on a small side table in the far corner. Gold looked at me and opened her hands.

'You take it,' I puffed, and sat thankfully into the armchair.

She walked to the table. 'It's a modern one, I'll put it on speaker.' She pressed a button and picked up the receiver. 'Hello?'

'Is Mr Hanson there?' It was a voice that I recognised but couldn't place.

'I'm sorry, he's not in. Can I take a message?'

'Yeah, just tell him Nevis is asking about him. I didn't tell him the address, but he knows about the warehouse.'

'Who did you say, Nevis?'

'Yeah, Ben Nevis – he'll know who I mean. Just tell him, right?'

'Right, and who shall I say called?'

'Jimmy, Jimmy Blunt – he'll know who I am.'

'Okay, Mr Blunt, I'll pass that on.'

The line went dead. Gold looked at me. 'Do you know a Jimmy Blunt?'

I nodded. 'Oh yes, I know a Jimmy Blunt.'

CHAPTER 30

We went down into the garden and dragged the bodies across to the door to the beach. It was secured to the wall by a chain and padlock fed through a hasp and staple. One bullet split the padlock which hung on the staple in two pieces as the chain fell to the ground. I pulled the door open.

'What do you have in mind for them?' asked Gold, pointing at the bodies. 'Dump them in the sea and let the tide take them away?'

I actually hadn't thought of that. 'No, it might wash them out and then back in again. I have a plan.'

'I hope it's not a Baldrick plan.'

She had complete faith in me as usual. I explained what I had in mind. The explanation was met with a perfunctory 'Okay, let's do it and get away from here.'

I waded out from the shore a few metres and grabbed the mooring rope of a twelve-foot motor boat with its outboard motor held above the water by a steel clip. Could be Hanson's, but I doubt it. My memory of him from the few times our paths crossed was of a man who kept his head down,under the radar, didn't call attention to himself. Probably the reason he is still alive and at the top of his nasty profession. He certainly wouldn't want to call attention to himself with an expensive boat making the locals wonder who he was, and where the money came from.

I pulled the motorboat as near the beach as I could without actually beaching it on the pebbles. One by one we lifted the bodies and put them into the boat neatly sitting next to each other on the two double seats. Gold passed me the two Semtex sticks and a fuse from the Burberry. I pushed them into the top pocket of Erdinger's jacket and pressed the fuse into one.

The way you drive a motorboat is much the same as a car: steering wheel, accelerator, clutch, gears and brake. The difference being it has just three gear stick positions: forward, neutral and reverse. Gold fetched a large, heavy rock from the beach which we jammed against the accelerator. I used a smaller one to smash the plastic cover of the ignition unit and cut the wire from the battery and the wire to the starter motor with my knife from my ankle sheath. When I connected the two wires, the starter motor would engage the engine and forward gear and start the propeller turning, and with the accelerator fully pressed down under the rock the boat would move forward fast. Last thing was to make sure which direction it moved fast in. I pushed the body of the goon in the driver's seat forward and pulled his arms through the steering wheel, holding it in a straight position. We pushed the boat out a few metres into the sea, Gold on one side, me on the other. I made sure it was pointing out into the estuary before I lifted the outboard motor off the clip and let it drop into the water.

'Ready?'

She nodded. 'Ready.'

I leant in, pushed the clutch pedal down and engaged the gear stick into the forward position. Then I snapped the Semtex fuse in Erdinger's top pocket. It would take thirty seconds for the acid to eat through the thin tube and heat the chemical mix that would burst into flame and explode the Semtex sticks which should send the whole package either up in the air or to the bottom of the sea in a million pieces. I pulled the two pieces of ignition wire together and the starter motor coughed into life, followed by the engine giving a roar as the propeller turned and the boat heading out into the estuary, picking up speed. We turned for the beach and stood and watched. That boat could move fast! It melted into the darkness of the water in the distance and it seemed an age passed. I began to worry that something had gone wrong with the fuse or the Semtex. I needn't have; the explosion lit up the whole of the estuary, with the fuel from the motorboat's tanks adding a fireball that rose into the air.

'Move.' Gold jabbed me in the side.

She was right, we had better make ourselves scarce. We got back to the car dripping from the knees down. She drove along the beach lane, lights out until we turned onto the road leading up and through the main area. All was still quiet, but people were pointing towards the beach area and hurrying that way. At the causeway the tide was out and we had to pull over and wait as two police cars with screaming sirens and flashing lights raced across from the mainland.

A mile along the Colchester road Gold pulled into a layby and we swapped the registration plates. If there was CCTV on Mersea Island that had picked up the Kia then it would not be picked up again. It's a basic action car thieves use to 'disappear' a car; the plates you use are copies of correct registrations for the make and year of the car, so any ANPR or police car checking it would find everything in order. Gilbert Charles has a lucrative sideline in providing them. I have two sets for my Range Rover; I don't know how many sets Gold has.

I relaxed once we hit the A12 and headed for London. I wondered what Hanson would have done if he had received Jimmy Blunt's call? My recollection of Hanson was that he didn't leave any loose ends, and I would qualify as a loose end.

I don't leave loose ends either, and Jimmy Blunt was certainly one of those.

CHAPTER 31

The Mersea Island boat explosion didn't make the national papers or Sky News. I checked the local paper, the East Anglian Times online over breakfast; nothing. The authorities probably put the explosion down to a boat malfunction. No body bits could have been found, or it would have made the local paper at least.

I rang Woodward.

He answered straight away. 'Good morning, Nevis. Good news, I hope?'

'Very good news – job done.'

'Erdinger?'

'With his son.'

'The body?'

'If you like oysters I'd avoid those from Essex for a while.'

He laughed. 'Aah, I did wonder whether that little episode in the Blackwater Estuary had anything to do with you, and what about Hanson?'

'We avoided contact. Clancy has an Interpol operation going and didn't want it compromised.'

'That's fine. Have you told him about Erdinger?'

'No, I'll leave that to you.'

'All right, I'll let him know that we have accomplished our objective and are now out of the picture.'

I liked the '*we*' bit, but decided not to comment. He continued.

'Just so you know, the far right yobbos the Terrorism Squad arrested at the Manchester Hotel have all been charged with membership of a proscribed organisation and attending an illegal meeting as such. They have been bailed to appear at court in a couple of weeks. They'll get a hefty fine or six months. The Pyramid units abroad have mostly been shut down by the local militia or police, so all in all a good result, Nevis. Any loose ends you can think of that might come back to bite us?'

'No, there's one loose end, but it's a personal one and I'll handle it.'

'All right, so, well done, Nevis. I will no doubt be in touch for your services in the future.'

Click, and he was gone. And that was that. I checked my bank account online. The money from MI6 was there except for the last day's payment. They pay daily, so that would be sent through later. I sent Gold her half and sent a

WhatsApp message telling her to check her account.

I had a couple of things to do. First I took an Uber to a jeweller I know in Hatton Garden, Solly Cohen. He's just like Gilbert Charles: posh premises, expensive suit, and a list of petty convictions as long as your arm. He smiled when I walked in.

'I was hoping you wouldn't come back.'

'That's nice.'

'You know I don't mean it, but the package you gave me to work on, oy vey!' He held up his hands in a gesture of amazement. 'Such quality I don't see every day.'

He knelt and opened one of two small safes bolted to the floor behind the counter and pulled out a small wrapped box and handed it to me.

'The bill?' I asked.

'If your lady friend likes it, then I give you a bill. If she doesn't, I re-work it for her and give you a bigger bill.' He laughed.

I nodded. 'Okay, I'm sure she will like it. I'll pop in next week and settle up.'

I left and hailed a black cab. I always split my journeys between Ubers and black cabs; makes it very difficult for anybody checking my movements at a later date.

‘Waterloo Station, please’

Whenever Gold drops me off it is either Waterloo Station or Victoria Station; that way neither of us knows where the other lives. So should the problem arise, nobody will be able to get my address from her or her address from me. The old gangster film line of *‘I’ll die before I tell you’* would be true.

I gave her mobile a call. She answered. ‘Yes, Ben?’

‘Got a few minutes?’

‘Yes.’

‘I’ll be in the Waterloo Station sheltered drop-off lane in ten minutes.’

‘Okay.’

****

I paid off the cab at the station and waited. It was only a ten minute walk to my apartment block from there. Gold’s Kia drew to a halt beside me and I got into the passenger seat.

‘Where to?’ she asked.

‘Nowhere,’ I said. ‘Here, I forgot to give you this.’ I handed over the small box. ‘That’s all. I’ll be in touch.’

She gave me a quizzical look as I opened the door and got out.

'Hang on... what...?'

Too late. I was gone, mixing into the crowds with a big smile on my face.

You have guessed it, haven't you, dear reader? Yes, the Angolan diamonds. Solly Cohen had made a gold necklace and spread half of them along it. Well, I hoped he had, that's what I told him to do. I had the other half. They were going into my safe deposit box at.... well, you don't expect me to tell you where, do you?

Oh, and Jimmy Blunt? He fell in front of a tube train at New Cross. Tragic, eh? The coroner said the autopsy report concluded that his prosthetic knee may have collapsed. Then again, he may have been pushed?

THE END

Thank you for buying this book. If you enjoyed it please leave a review or rating on Amazon as that would mean an awful lot to me. Thank you in advance.

To see more books in this series and others in my back catalogue check my Amazon page. I don't have a website, not enough time.

Take care and stay safe!

DCS Palmer books

Future Riches
The Felt Tip Murders
A Killer is Calling
Poetic Justice
Loot
I'm With The Band
Burning Ambition
Take Away Terror
Ministry of Death
The Bodybuilder
Succession
The Black Rose
Laptops Can Kill
Screen 4
Underneath The Arches

Ben Nevis and the Gold Digger Series

Turkish Delight

National Treasure
Chinese Takeaway
Double Trouble
The Pyramid

True Crime
London Crime 1930s-2021 (factual)
UK Serial Killers 1930-2021 (factual)
UK Killers Vol 1.1900-1921 (factual)
UK Killers Vol 2.
UK Killers Vol 3.
American Killers. Vol 1. Alabama.
American Killers. Vol 2. Arizona

Bidder Beware (Comedy)
Fred Karno biography